Social Graces

Social Graces

By
Malinda M. Hall

CREATIVE ARTS BOOK COMPANY
Berkeley • California

Social Graces is published by Donald S. Ellis
and distributed by Creative Arts Book Company

For information contact:
Creative Arts Book Company
833 Bancroft Way
Berkeley, California 94710
(800) 848-7789

ISBN 0-88739-289-X
Library of Congress Catalog Number 99-63871

Printed in the United States of America

Dedicated to C. Mike,
who made me get on the plane

Social Graces

The headaches had been coming with more frequency, and they seemed to gain in intensity until they reached a crescendo of discomfort and pain. Sometimes, as promised by the medical encyclopedia of television, an advertised over-the-counter pill did its job, and the headache was gone. Lately, that had not been the case, and a rainbow of pills couldn't touch the pain. When her head hurt, the room spun. When the room spun, she couldn't move. Lethargy and somnolence wrapped her like a dank, heavy blanket. If her head would quit hurting, she could wear the lethargy to bed and maybe sleep. It seemed that reading a book, or working in the garden, or taking a walk would work out some of the pain, but her body wouldn't allow her to make the first step toward any productive action. She couldn't work because she hurt. She couldn't rest because she hurt. She hurt because she couldn't rest.

When it blew, it was volcanic, rocking her body, blinding her eyes, tearing her ears—Mt. St. Helens in compressed time.

Get to the phone. . .call 911. . .call. . .someone. . .come, please come.

One

I WAS LATE—AGAIN.

If I were an ingenious liar, I probably could have framed a wonderfully original excuse based on the rain. Starting last night and continuing into this morning, it had come down so densely it looked like sheets of plastic. I could have prevaricated a beautiful traffic tie-up, which wouldn't be difficult to believe because the highways and streets were perpetually being reconstructed. The only hole in that lie was that the sheety rain had been with us continually for a good three weeks, and the traffic jams were becoming fewer by the day as Northern Californians got their driving workout and built up resistance to streets and highways doused by the hard rain. The other flaw in making excuses was that this staff was beyond believing anything I could come up with because I had been late one hundred and two days last year. Courtesy of Genevieve Gould, one of my co-workers, all of us were privy to that information because she had kept track of all the employees' tardies and absences and announced the total at one of our Tuesday staff meetings. Now the office had a betting pool going with each staff member, except Charles who knew nothing of this, estimating how many days I would be late this year. From the scuttlebutt, someone stood to win a big pot.

As I rushed in the door, it seemed that the desk said, "She did it to me again."

Exhaling a shallow pant, I asked the 'desk' what it meant. A sleek blonde head thrust upward, and Dolly, the agency's office manager, proceeded to explain with a rueful smile.

"The court called and referred an apparent case of parent abuse. Since Leticia is good with geriatrics, I thought the case should go to her, so I checked with Charles who agreed. I called

1

Leticia at home and left a message for her on her answering machine to get back to me. I left a note on her desk, her e-mail and her voice mail, and I left word with as many of the staff as I could find to tell her to contact me. She and I finally connected and set up an appointment for her to go to the senior residence and meet the referral. I finalized all that and left word with her again at all those places. This morning at eight, guess who calls?"

"Well, it has to be Leticia or the court, right?"

"Right. The court. Leticia didn't show for the appointment. When I talked to her at nine, finally, she said she hadn't received any word of the appointment time. Now how in the world can that be when I've talked to her off and on for a week about this thing, and I've left confirmation at all those places when I had it set?" asked Dolly.

Cute, petite Dolly was model perfect yet more nourished than most of them. Although young, she was mature in competence, which she proved daily by artfully juggling schedules for all of us in the office. She was usually calm, so to be this upset, someone must be riding her very hard.

"She always does those things to me," she pouted. "She always sets it up, so I think I'm the one who made the mistake. This time I did what you suggested: I put the confirmation in her e-mail and in Charles' e-mail, and I wrote it on her calendar. That way, it's not my mistake; it's hers, and it's her problem. It's sure good she works well with those clients because that's how she stays on the good side of Charles. I think anyone else would have fired her, but she's so slick the way she butters him up."

She vented her anger a little more and, finally, began to calm down. As she did, she remembered, "By the way, Charles wants to see you immediately. He didn't seem too pleased when I told him you weren't here yet, and, frankly, I didn't cover well for you this time. I think the Leticia thing is really stuck in my craw. I just don't know how she can stay one step ahead of everyone else, so she looks great while we look like incompetent schmucks."

Dolly has an appreciation for each person's job and never lets her efficiency demean someone else's work. Because she looks out for all of us, she manages to keep the office running smoothly by keeping office one-upmanship buried in the nether world of lost files. That is, until Leticia has her way with our schedules. Then it's hard for anyone, even Dolly, to unravel the tangle she gets us in.

I commiserated with Dolly, "The old CYA, cover your ass." I really needed to get to the issue at hand, which involved my boss, so, dreading the answer, I asked, "Did Charles say what he wanted?"

"Does he ever come out and say directly what he wants? I already told you he was asking about you, and I didn't cover well. I bet you can guess though."

With an inward groan, I meandered back to Charles' offices. Shoot, if he's going to ream me out for being late again, why rush?

It wasn't hard to draw out the walk because of the way our offices had been set up. Rather than use a standard office complex in a high rise, the board of directors had elected to lease a converted warehouse in one of the new soft industrial areas of town. Rent was cheaper, which was good for the budget; offices were ground level, which was good for our non-ambulatory clients; rooms were spacious and windows were plentiful, which was good for staff morale.

There was also the added factor that Pleasant Creek was successfully creating itself in the image of San Francisco. This was done with the basic building blocks of skyscrapers, not too high, so the view of Mt. Diablo would only be enhanced in a contemporary frame. Soft industries such as finance, high-tech and computer glossed that image with a patina of finesse. Sprinkle all that with gourmet restaurants, high-end shopping, and creative art galleries and museums, and the elegance of San Fran was replicated. Therefore, putting our offices out of the city center gave us lower rent but still maintained our can-do image because we were in a get-things-done city.

Leaving the waiting room of green, marigold, and taupe, with its comfortable waiting chairs, I wandered through the long hallway, off of which were offices with the added benefit of windows for each staff member. Continuing down the hallway, I passed the file room, conference room, the kitchen, and dining complex before coming to the end of the very long hall which was the exit to the back parking lot. Perpendicular to that door on the adjoining wall was the open door to Charles' offices which projected beyond the hallway with a view of the employee parking lot only an administrator could appreciate. Not only were Charles and Betty, his secretary, able to monitor the back door for safety purposes, they also had a splendid view of the comings and goings of employees.

Betty acknowledged my entry with a raise of an eyebrow and dialed the intercom to announce my presence to Charles as I took a seat. Betty's been around the agency since it started, so she knows it better than anyone. She's nice, she's thorough, she's telepathic. It's easier for her not to begin any kind of conversation because then she might have to talk too long to too many people about too much drivel, and then she couldn't be thorough.

Sitting there with Betty efficiently and silently processing words and brandishing files, I had a chance to think about what Dolly had said earlier. She was right. Charles never came out and explained exactly what he was after. His style of administration was to give a general idea of what he had in mind and then let others fill in the details. It must be effective because in the last four years, he and his Ph.D. in Sociology had taken a small debt-ridden, bleeding-heart social work agency to the pinnacle of community service agencies. That meant that he, through fundraisers, sliding-scale fee for services, and charity organization hobnobbing, not to mention a few lucrative government and HMO contract services, had put the agency into a profit. If he could have, he probably would have issued stock, gone public, and turned social work into a superstore delivery system.

He had also hired three graduate-level social workers and had quadrupled the caseload. That made the board of directors happy, it made the city council happy, and, supposedly, made the community freer of social ills. Exact explanation of his plans and sharing credit for his superhuman exploits would, presumably, have detracted from his rock-solid reputation of charming glibness and single-handed accomplishment. If he uncloaked his hidden agenda, he might offend either side of the fence he so carefully straddled. But, to his credit, he did handle people well, and he did get the job done expertly. Leticia served his purposes in that regard because she was careful to make him look good.

Hiring those three graduate-level people put the three old-timers a little to the outside of his plans because we weren't the image of the young, technically advanced, and-up-to-date organization he wanted the world to see the agency as. He had to put up with us, however, as we cumulatively had eighty years with Community Services, Inc. As Charles brought the agency out of the red and more into the pink, the board of directors raised its standard of composition by commanding a higher level of the social strata. To reflect this tonier image, the name of the agency was changed to the Community Action Group, and, of course, with this name change came a new location, a different logo, other stationery and a change of policy. Even some of society's dilemmas had changed. Now added to dealing with alcoholism, child welfare, and domestic abuse were caseloads that included drug abuse, HIV/AIDS and homelessness components. Much to Charles' chagrin, the only thing that hadn't changed was we three old-timers. He never seemed to appreciate the fact that the years of experience we brought to the agency, in some ways, were more valuable than any advanced degrees our young social workers had. Perhaps he could feel the pressure of all that experience in light of his youth; after all, he was only thirty-three. Maybe we emanated superior airs around him and didn't realize it. Perhaps we used body language or voice tone that indicated a lack of respect for advanced degrees.

Two

TIME WAS DOING THE MILITARY THING AND MARCHING on, and, yet, I continued to wait for the summons of Charles, who, at this point, was wasting my day even more than I had by being late. I had just about talked myself into excusing his myopic attitude toward his non-advanced degreed people when looking out toward the hallway, I decided Charles might have a legitimate reason for wishing away the half of his staff with most of the experience.

Genevieve Gould, self-appointed keeper of schedules and lives and one of us old-timers, strode into the reception area of Charles' office with Jill Amos, one of the advanced degreed youngsters. These two women had gone to the same college, at different times, of course. When Genevieve learned of their college connection, in her mind, that connected them up like Velcro, and she immediately designated herself Jill's best friend in the office. If Genevieve's on the prowl, it must be Monday because that was her information update session.

"Well, dear, how was your weekend?" she purred as she slid into the chair next to me. The coif color of the week was pale green, very similar to that of a competitive swimmer, whose hair had suffered chlorine overload, except Genevieve's body belied the fact she swam or exercised in any way.

It's wise to take Genevieve's questions at less than face value. Over the years, she has demonstrated her questions are asked not so much out of concern for her friends, but because she wants to derive information for gossip fests. Catalog shopping could use Genny's mind as a model of organization for minute information. She had a cerebral file on everyone in the office, not to mention her clients, and constantly updated it. Like most activities, this could be bad, or it could be good. Good for elusive information about clients, bad for the rest of our privacy.

I told her, "Same old routine, Gen. I went home, cleaned, washed the clothes, and mowed the lawn. The dog and I took a couple of long power walks, and on Saturday I went to a barbecue at my daughter and son-in-law's house."

"Did they have anyone interesting for you to meet?" she wheedled, batting her eyelashes. "I do hope they're still out there looking for a companion for you. You just can't sit at home all the time and mope about being single. It's not healthy. It's just not good to sit home like you do. I've found in my experience people need to have other people. We are gregarious by nature, and that includes in the home. You will probably need counseling yourself if you don't find a steady companion soon," she dripped, dripped, dripped like the proverbial faucet. How many times I've heard this!

Genevieve's husband divorced her about the same time I divorced mine. Then, we had much in common and spent many dinners comparing and contrasting our situations. We went to lots of tearjerker movies and jerked lots of tears to deal with the emotional fracture we had both undergone. But, as with all tragedies, time healed, and the fracture started to knit. Genevieve found a new companion, as in male, and, eventually, married him. I didn't, and still haven't. Part of the reason lies in the fact I still miss my husband. Much of it is because I don't want to have to spend my holidays with someone else's children and listen to the idyllic memories of their youth while they won't want to hear about my own kids.

"No, Genevieve, they didn't. After the last one, they figured they'd quit playing the matchmaker bit. With their last choice, they ran out of topics with which to fill the conversational lulls after he completed his account of river rafting down the Colorado River and dog sledding in Alaska. It's hard to compete with that kind of event-filled conversation."

Pausing to let her file away that information, I added, "Besides the guy was fifteen years younger than me. Can you imagine me dog sledding in Alaska?"

While Genny paused, an almost unheard of thing to occur when she had you cornered, Jill chuckled and even Betty smiled. Jill's calm, fluid movements imparted to those around her a serene safety which was a nice balance to Genny's staccato lurching, and she was just about to say something when Genny lurched into, "Frankly, yes, it would be right up your alley. An old woman traipsing through Alaska behind a bunch of mutts. You'd probably catch pneumonia, and then, well, who knows, then you might, oh, I don't know, die or something." She swept her conclusion into the air with a flourish.

Leaving no time to interject a defense, let alone a retort, she launched into her recurrent lecture, "You know, Louisa, you really must get awfully lonely not having a *man* around the house. If I hadn't had my Sid yesterday to help me hang the curtain rod, I never would have gotten those curtains up."

"Yes, you would. You would have called me. I've told you a million times you have the ability to do household maintenance yourself. There is a great fallacy in the world that women are incapable of picking up a screwdriver and hammer and using them. It's great to have some company while doing those jobs. It's even fun sometimes to do them together. But, Genevieve, the poor helpless little me nonsense has got to go. At your age, it's unbecoming."

Ignoring the comments and the speaker, she heaved out of the chair, pointedly placed a file she was carrying on Betty's desk, took Jill's arm, and escorted her out of the office. We could hear her describing to Jill the blue and white curtains she and Sid had hung.

As Betty rerouted the file on her desk, the intercom rang, and Charles requested my presence.

As he always does when a woman enters the room, Charles stood. His impeccable manners are only exceeded by his impeccable clothing. Charles is probably the only social worker in the world who dresses as if he were a corporate attorney planning to spend all day in court. Today he wore a nubby charcoal on white plaid suit that yielded a gray color, beautifully accented by the gold cufflinks and yellow patterned heavy silk tie. His hairdresser, his manicurist, and his gym trainer maintained his gentleman's appearance to perfection.

"Thank you, Mrs. Daniel, for responding to my request to see me first thing this morning. I know the hour is getting on, and you must have much paperwork to do, so I won't keep you long. We really do need to discuss your schedule."

He was gearing up for the standard lecture about case reports. He also had an oration on being late in the morning although he tends not to berate most of us too much for that. He knows our caseloads can keep us working until late evening. In keeping his personnel skills honed, he has designated each one of us to receive his homilies on good work and office habits. I am often the recipient of the value of being on time. Not that I don't deserve it. Why not fill that extra ten minutes before I have to leave for an appointment with a small job? The problem only occurs when the ten minutes stretches to fifteen or twenty which can impact scheduling. I figured long ago if I can squeeze an extra five to ten minutes out of each waking hour, I've added two extra hours to the twenty-four most of us are allotted.

Onward Charles. "Now, Mrs. Daniel, as we've discussed before, to keep up our accreditation with the state, we must always have current and up-to-date reports. As good a counselor as you are in dealing with people, you really do need to continue to refine your recordkeeping skills. Now, if you were always in the office at the required hour, you would not have difficulty in keeping your records. It is a professional duty to be where one is expected when one is expected. If I were consistently late as you are, this agency would not be able to service the community in the glowing manner it does."

Charles is efficient today; he's managed to combine both lectures in one shot.

"Charles, as usual, when we discuss this, you are right," my voice mirrored his professionalism. "I only have three people to see in the office today. I will stay until the cases are completed and on your desk tonight."

"That would be excellent, Mrs. Daniel. I do appreciate your cooperative nature," he said. He seemed to be expecting a confrontation and appeared relieved it didn't occur. Poor Charles. I suppose if I had to administer to employees who kept schedules like mine, I might wish away half the staff, too.

So, that's how I spent the day. The reports got done, and the cases were placed on Betty's desk by six. Dolly set up some conference calls with a few professionals and court officers, and we completed some detail work for a few of the clients. Feeling almost giddy because the tedium was completed, and I could ignore paperwork for another few days, I drove home and was greeted at the door by Woofy, my pet project, literally, from the animal shelter.

Woofy is the most reliable companion in my life. If I'm happy, he's happy. If I'm angry, he's happy. If I'm despondent or just lonely, he's happy. And, he's always there.

Three

BECAUSE WOOFY BECOMES A CANINE PROJECTILE WHEN he greets me, I step into the door off-center. This way he does not wind me too much, nor do we end up in a furry heap on the garage floor. After opening the door, we greeted each other, and the phone rang. The answering machine did not win this race, but I was out of breath as I said hello.

"Louisa, you need to get over here right now," Leticia never identifies herself. She assumes, usually correctly, her distinctive, low voice will be recognized.

"Leticia, I just got home. Can you wait until I eat and straighten up the house?" I knew this would annoy her. Leticia forgets individuals' routines don't always coincide with hers.

"Well, hurry it up. I need some advice now, and you're probably the most objective person I know, so you're the best advisor I can come up with—and the most available."

"Give me an hour, and I'll be there."

"I guess so. Hurry up, though. I don't have all night to wait for you." And then Leticia added a muffled afterthought, "Please." As she is not one to use the polite words that oil life's doings, the 'please' only added to the urgency of her request.

The fact she would even have me come to her apartment was another indication she felt she needed help. No one I knew had ever been invited to her place. Leticia had hung up before I could get directions, but I located an old staff directory. In zealous efficiency, Dolly had created our first directory when she started working at the office. The only clinker was she had forgotten to ask all staffers if it was alright to publish address information. It's an honest mistake. How was she to know Leticia placed that data in the same category as her ATM pin number? Dolly, convinced by Leticia her job was in great jeopardy, scampered around and destroyed all copies except the one I never told her I had. So, after whisking a frozen entrée from the freezer and nuking it, I studied the map to locate her residence, Surprisingly enough on a social worker's salary, she lived in an exclusive area of the county. Reading was going to have been my fare for the evening, but Leticia, who prefers to demand rather than ask, had requested my help. Besides, it would be a coup among the office staff to be the first one on my block to see her place. My curiosity and her entreaty greatly hastened the dinner hour.

Woofy loves to ride in the car. The rain of the day had dissipated, so it made sense to take him with me. Hearing the jingle of the keys, he ran to the door and wagged himself silly with excitement. Woofy is my own American Kennel Club, a little Black lab, some German shepherd, a bit of Irish retriever, the best of breeds all rolled into one. As he perched himself on the backseat, I set out for the half-hour drive and thought about Leticia.

Dolly said she never did contact the hospital. Leticia is unreliable for appointments, but she always has some legitimate sounding excuse or outright lie as to why she can't make her set times. To date, I hadn't heard of her ever shirking responsibility so much that she hadn't completed an assignment. Maybe that could be why she called. Maybe she had an anxiety attack about missing the hospital appointment and letting the agency down.

On the other hand, Leticia had never let what other people thought of her bother her. Even when she apologized for frustrating someone's plans, she never sounded wholehearted in her request for forgiveness. She never owned to the fact that she had made a mistake. Co-workers would hint, cajole and openly insist one of her actions caused a problem, but she would smile her tight-lipped grimace, look them in the eye and lie about the circumstances leading to the problem. It was unlikely she had become anxious. Probably she had some plan to manipulate one of us to be her excuse, and, somehow, it was to involve me.

My county houses so many bedroom communities that many people don't even know our towns and cities by name. It's easier to just say I live in Contra Costa County rather than try to name my town of residence. Since before the Caldecott Tunnel poked its fingers through the Oakland Hills, Oaklanders and San Franciscans used to escape the cold August days by trekking over the hills to the inland heat of Contra Costa. Still standing from the early twentieth century are many vintage summer cottages, since remodeled into glorious showplaces that are grouped into trendy communities.

To one of these former resort villages was where I now headed. After winding up and down its narrow, picturesque village roads and finding myself lost a few times, I finally pulled up to Leticia's condominium complex. I rolled the windows down slightly and told Woofy to watch and not bark. Of course, he started barking as soon as I locked the car door. Figuring this was to be my exercise for the day, I puffed up the stairs to Leticia's third floor unit after walking down the many steps into the small crevasse where her condos had been built. It seems the more elite a town, the narrower and curvier the roads. The classier the home, the higher on the hill or the lower in the valley it must be.

There aren't many true, natural beauties in the world. With make-up, nip and tuck surgery and no fat/low fat eating, most of us can disguise our natal shortcomings. Leticia didn't need to disguise anything. Her matte-finished face was not make-up; it was real. Her full lips and Greco-Roman nose were genetic endowments. Her shiny dark hair was not dye. When she opened her door, her gray eyes, made more arresting by the golden halo surrounding each pupil, glistened, but the flawless skin, tonight, was marred. She had tried to mask the green and blue swelling on her face but not successfully.

Because she is a very covert person, none of us knows anything substantial about Leticia. Whatever facts she revealed came in short bursts of enlightenment. Sometimes, when discussing a case, she would exhibit empathy only a fellow participant could understand. Given that the less known about a person, the more we'd like to fill in with gossip and innuendoes had been demonstrated repeatedly in Leticia's case. If the talkfest dragged, someone would invariably bring up Leticia, and someone else, usually Genevieve, would fan the flames of half-truths into fiery gossip. In my infrequent forays into the lunchroom, I'd heard ambient tidbits about Leticia. I had heard about her latest squeeze because the rest of the staff loved to lay open Leticia's life the way they saw it and had constructed her boyfriend into a pulsating battering ram ready to strike at any minute. Her bruises validated the lunchroom buzz.

She stood there without saying anything, so I opened with, "The boyfriend do that to you? I thought you told people he's sober. Why do you run around with someone who beats you?"

"Yes, but, Louisa, you can't possibly begin to understand," she said as her hand wandered up to the tender spot and barely touched it.

"Yes, I understand. I understand that he's off the wagon, and you still want to defend him. You're a social worker. You, of all people, should know what working with alcoholism is. You're giving him excuses and enabling him to continue the alcoholism. Other people can plead ignorance, you can't. You're supposed to be a professional. Come on, Leticia, do you need me to tell you what to do?"

"No, I don't want that. He's still on the wagon; he's been working with me, so, of course, he'll stay sober. It's something you don't understand. There was no way I could come to work today. I assume you're angry about my missing the appointment at the hospital."

"Me? Why should I be angry? Did you call me here to do your dirty work and deliver an apology to Dolly? And Charles?

You clean up your own messes. It's your problem, not mine. By your missing the appointment, Dolly's the one who looks foolish, and since she's the office manager of the agency, it looks irresponsible."

Leticia said angrily, "Come on, Louisa, I said you don't understand, and I mean you don't understand. You can't come into my home and start yelling at me."

I railed at her some more, "Hold it. Leticia, you're the one who asked—no, *told* me to come. I didn't spend a half hour in the car just to take some twilight cruise up narrow roads that present a wonderful opportunity to drive off a hill and break my neck.

"Charles is going to split his gut. We can fudge intraoffice doings, but you know when there's a mistake made public, he goes into apoplexy. I sure don't want to be in your shoes. I understand why you couldn't come to work. You could have made another excuse like you always do and told some half-truth about running into a door or something."

Here was this woman who was as beautiful as she was self-assured, and she'd tied up with some asshole who got his strokes in life by backhanding her. It was incomprehensible because she didn't exhibit the defining aspect of a battered woman's syndrome: letting someone else demand that she do anything other than what she wished to do. She never let anyone at work walk over her. She had a Masters in Social Work, was an outstanding counselor, and she'd hooked up with a batterer for a boyfriend. Beating of women, children and animals sends snakes up my back anyway. To think this woman had the expertise in dealing with the subject and still succumbed to it made me disgustedly furious. I opened my mouth to machine gun her again with my fury, but she interrupted me.

"Okay, I deserve all that. But, Louisa, you—oh, all right I'll talk to the paralegal. I know her pretty well, and I'll fix it. I'll make it up to Dolly somehow. I just couldn't face the situation because I knew tongues would start wagging," she said sheepishly and winced slightly. She knew I knew what she was really saying and whom she was really talking about, and, at that moment, my heart went out to her because all that gossip about her eventually got back to her. From the look on her face, it bothered her, maybe more than we realized.

"Now, look, I need help from you," she said brusquely as the more familiar Leticia returned. "There's a situation at work that must be handled with sensitivity. I'm not sure where I can go, but you are fairly discreet. You tend to keep your mouth shut. It's a strange combination of—" She broke off her preamble when the phone rang.

"Stay, Louisa. I'll make this call short, and then I can explain what I need you to do."

The phone call gave me a chance to visually devour an exquisite living area. The tapestry camelback sofa of muted taupes and grays accented a pair of matching striped charcoal and off-white club chairs. Marbleized flooring in the same monochromatic grays and blacks was set off by the glass and metal table in the center of the room. Black leather empire chairs were placed close enough to this area to be either drawn into a conversation or to become part of the inlaid wood gaming table. The upholstery on the dining room chairs carried the tapestry of the sofa into the eating area that was bordered at the ceiling with a valence of patterned wallpaper.

Interestingly enough, as extremely tasteful and stunning as the rooms were, there was nothing personalized about them. There were no family portraits or photos; there were no magazines or books. There were no discarded shoes or sweaters laying about, no curios or mementos. Anything placed on the furniture surfaces was done strictly to match the décor, just as was done in a hotel room. Leticia's condo matched her demeanor. It was the height of style, but wore little emotion, just like her.

Yet, even in spite of her use, or misuse, of her co-workers and her seemingly emotionless life, she was likable. Well, maybe not likable, but able to be respected. Leticia couldn't be included as one of my friends because, except for tonight, we never had contact outside of the office. I'd even include Genevieve among my friends because we had been through so much over the years. But I could really respect Leticia because of her wonderful quality of truly caring for the down and out. Of all the social workers in the office, she was the one who would get under the skin of her clients. She would find out what they wanted and needed and try to work through the red tape of bureaucracy to get it for them. All of us in the office had seen her tackle and harass an agency until she got what she demanded for the needs of her client. Then she'd go to the agency workers who were ready to crucify her and cajole and sweet-talk until they would trumpet her praises to the next county. Her adept manipulation in the cause of our clients was seen as good and beneficial; however, when it was used on us, it was annoying and brought discontent to our staff.

The phone conversation continued, but I couldn't hear what was being said because Leticia was inside the next room. On Leticia's forehead was an almost imperceptible frown. If I hadn't glanced at her just at that time, I might not have seen it. She noticed me looking at her, put her hand on the phone and said, "Louisa, this is going to take longer than I thought. You may go home now. I'll see you tomorrow at staffing."

With that she turned away from me to the phone, and I let myself out.

As blunt as Leticia's send-off had been, Woofy's greeting made up for it. Hoisting himself to a sitting position, tongue lolling, his brown eyes looked relieved that I made it back. Having been abandoned once before, Woofy would probably never feel assured it couldn't happen again.

Four

IT WAS FORTUNATE EMILY CALLED WHEN SHE DID because my internal alarm didn't work the next morning, and I had forgotten to set the clock. Leticia, her frowning face and her exquisite, but sterile, home wove themselves in and out of my dreams causing a fitful sleep. Emily or David, her husband, call almost everyday on the pretext of telling me about the grand-daughters and their latest escapades. Over the years they must have realized I know they are really calling to make sure I have weathered my ten-year status as a single, older woman. I appreciate their efforts to disguise this concern; it means my dignity being intact is important to them. One of their ways of maintaining this dignity is calling at the earliest hours of the day or at bedtime in the evening. This way none of my peers can track the regularity of their check-ups on me. Emily related yesterday's tales of Jojo and Lulie, nicknames derived from Josephine and Louisa, with greater gusto and longer telling time than usual. Giving her the verbal pat on the head young parents seek, I told her I was running late and raced to the office after dressing.

Even though he has come to expect it, Charles still can-not hide his annoyance when I bounce in late to a Tuesday staff meeting. He doesn't even ask for excuses anymore. My giving varying ones bores the staff and takes time from the meeting. Unusual as it was, this time I was not the latest staff member. Leticia came in fifteen minutes after I had settled in and was already breathing at a normal rate. Charles did ask her where she had been because she usually comes in to work before any-one else. This is another way of making sure no one invades her privacy by asking questions about her time away from the office. She gave a noncommittal response about a long phone

21

call keeping her up very late, but she said nothing about my coming to her home.

Charles closed the conversation with, "I hope it wasn't long distance," to which we all gave a polite chuckle.

Leticia looked around the room, spotted the only empty chair next to Jill, sat down, and picked through her briefcase. Jill then exaggeratedly gathered her papers, put them in her brief-case, and got out of her seat. She walked to the other side of the room and moved a chair to a space near Herb Engle, another staff member.

As Jill maneuvered this, Genevieve, who was now sitting beside Leticia, turned to her and said, "Did you know you have a smudge on your cheek?" When she reached up to brush the "smudge" away, Leticia pulled back and said sharply, "Don't touch me!"

In the ensuing, awkward silence, some people looked at Genevieve; others looked at Leticia. Most fidgeted with pencils or looked down at notes as if reviewing them.

Leticia glared at Gen who then said, "Well, well, Jill, you certainly are better off than some others in this room. I've told you, repeatedly, to stay away from him for just this reason. Now, aren't you relieved you listened to me? That could just as easily have been you showing up with bruises."

If the room had needed a paint job that day, it would have to be red; the collective embarrassment was that colorful.

Charles, of the impeccable manners, stepped into the middle of the room and, pretending this incident had not occurred, continued his discussion of the "Jail-Bail" which was the main topic of today's meeting. In the never-ending quest for creative and resourceful fundraising ideas, jail-bails are arriving on the scene. As new jails are built and before they are opened for business, local celebrities gather for a gala event. They show up in their designer evening wear, eat gourmet din-ners in the mess hall, allow themselves to be locked in a cell and sit there until they are auctioned out of it. The auction's pro-ceeds, or "bail money", is then given to the charity or non-profit organization for which funds are being raised. It was a hopeful way to open a jail. Why not whitewash for a day a building that will be a monument to human frailties and misery for the remainder of its existence?

It sounded like a reasonable fundraiser. We have been through many in our years in business. This was being organized by the county supervisors for the agencies in the county. Each community agency had been asked to provide help, and the net profit was then to be divided among those participating agencies. Because each agency would supply many volunteers, each of us would only have to spend a few hours doing a job that evening and then could socialize the remainder of the time.

As Charles provided more details, my concentration lagged, and I ruminated on the incident involving Leticia, Genevieve, and Jill. Jill's smooth face was pinched and gray. Leticia stared serenely at Charles in an apparent attitude of listening. Genevieve's head moved between Jill and Leticia's seats slowly like a spectator at a tennis match. The rest of the staff was listening to Charles at about the same level as I. Herb fiddled with his pencil, and Gladys Eng doodled on the Jail-Bail information sheet.

Charles must have realized he lost us because he closed the meeting shortly after that by having Betty pass around a clipboard with jobs listed to which we could assign ourselves. Jill signed her name, got up, and was the first one out of the room. Leticia slowly gathered her papers to be the last one out.

Five

GENEVIEVE AND I WALKED OUT OF THE MEETING behind Charles. As I opened my mouth to get her take on the meeting, a blond man came up to Charles and asked if he might talk with him. Charles grabbed his hand, shook it with gusto and clapped him on the back as though he were greeting the Publisher's Clearing House rep telling him he'd won the sweepstakes.

"I thought you'd have your sister with you. It's great to see you," Charles said as he escorted him to this office.

"Who it that?" I asked.

Genevieve squinted at him and said, "I think that must be Mrs. Streng's son."

"Mrs. Streng on our board of directors?" I asked.

"The very same. You know she had a fairly severe stroke? Her children decided she wasn't getting proper care at the convalescent home, so her son dropped everything to take care of her. I believe the daughter is still working outside the home, though.

"The son brought his mother home, equipped the house with all kinds of aids for stroke patients and now oversees all her services. They came to the agency on the advice of Dr. Cannaughton, the mother's doctor. Charles assigned Leticia to the case, and she gives advice as to whom Mrs. Streng should go for services. Sometimes she helps the children by taking care of Mrs. Streng if they have to go out. Leticia said she can hardly communicate, the stroke was so devastating. At first, they thought she would be okay because she was always so healthy. Now they think it's much worse because she hasn't relearned anything—no speech, no writing, no physical skills, nothing."

25

In the creation of a Board of Directors for a non-profit organization, a balance of people having expertise, money, and clout is sought. Mrs. Streng was one of those rare people who had all three. The money came from a combination of family resources and her late arbitrageur husband; the expertise came from her years of volunteer community work; her clout came from a combination of the other two qualities tempered by her tact and presence. She was easy to approach when we worked on a project and willingly gave whatever she had to the project to facilitate its completion. At some point in her life, she had decided she had received so many blessings that she needed to return some of them, and she had spent the last thirty years or so doing just that. She sat on several agency boards besides ours. She didn't give just money; she volunteered her time, her house, and her skills. In spite of exhaustive efforts and care given to the people in her volunteer work, she seemed to retain a serene elegance to every challenge presented her.

She never cut short anyone talking with her no matter how inane the speaker. When presented with a problem, she analyzed, summarized, and tackled it with the tenacity of a champion athlete. It's inspiring to watch the Mrs. Strengs of the world. They don't place themselves at the forefront, yet they are always there. They don't have to inflate their abilities because those around them seek them out with the knowledge that productive action will be taken. They have a dignified self-confidence that imparts to others assurance and respect.

And, now, that regal carriage had been decimated by a stroke. How long can serenity lie huddled in a hospital crib? Does it, too, become a host for the parasitic IV needles and hospital paraphernalia that, ironically, are designed to make the body strong, but make dignity weak? It was a shocking sadness to hear about Mrs. Streng's stroke, but it was a comfort to know she had children who cared enough to take her out of the convalescent home and give her personal care. Hopefully, that would hasten her recovery.

However, I was still curious about Jill and Leticia and the scene in the staff room. So I asked our resident encyclopedia, Genevieve, why she thought Jill was so rude to Leticia.

"Rude?" she exploded, "she wasn't rude. Why should she want to sit next to that woman who took her boyfriend, the love of her life? Leticia knows Jill doesn't want anything to do with her. Poor Jill has been hurt so badly."

I didn't think anyone "took" anyone away from someone, so the childishness of her words cautioned me to diplomacy. "But, Gen," I said, "they are grown adults and can make decisions on their own. No one can 'take someone away'. They have to take themselves away."

"Look, Louisa, I know you have trouble with men and have sworn them off, so you don't care to remember how they are. You have to constantly play up to them and make them think they have a computer mind, a Mr. Universe body and a Scrooge McDuck bank account. Leticia knows how to do all that. She also doesn't like Jill, so she went after her boyfriend, just out of spite."

Her analysis of my situation was off target, but I let it pass and continued to press her. After all, if her viewpoint of my life was skewed, perhaps she had misread Jill's life also.

I asked, "Genny, just what guy are we talking about?"

"Leticia just came in and took him. It happened so fast. One minute Jill was telling me about their weekend, and the next, she said they had broken it off. It wasn't until a few days later that Jill saw him go off with Leticia in her car after work. Then she knew. She knew …"

"Genevieve!" I interrupted. "Answer my question. Who is the boyfriend? What kind of person is he?"

"Oh, Louisa, you're so impatient. I'm trying to tell you. It's Kelly, you know, that lowlife who's always hanging around here after work. Blond guy, big, used to be really good looking. Then when you get to know him, you realize he's a jerk, and he's not so good looking. He drinks, and I wouldn't be surprised if he does drugs. Makes you wonder what Leticia is doing with him, doesn't it? She acts like she's so perfect, you'd think anyone around her would have to be that way, too. She's so cold; I just can't even imagine having to spend more than twenty minutes with someone who looks down on everyone else like she does."

After a pause, Gen answered her own question wistfully, "She sure is beautiful, though."

"So is Jill," I said, to which Gen nodded.

"Are you sure that's what happened? How do you know Leticia doesn't like Jill? Leticia treats all of us pretty much the same. I heard she was helping some guy on her own time; maybe this is the guy. Maybe Leticia is just what he needed. Maybe she could get him to get help when Jill couldn't."

"No, Louisa, you have it all wrong—again. Leticia passes that off that she got him into a substance abuse program. I think she's just saying that because Jill did try to get him into a program and couldn't. Obviously, it didn't do any good. Look at Leticia; he's knocking her around. He didn't even do that to Jill, at least, not that she told me. I bet he's still drinking, and now it's gotten worse." She was almost gloating.

"It seems hard to believe professionals would condone behavior in their own lives when they won't condone it in their clients' lives. These women are good social workers," I argued.

"Yes, Louisa, but they are also women. He's always around here waiting. Jill knows he's looking for Leticia. You think you have all the answers, Louisa. How can you possibly dare to suppose what has happened among those three young people?"

"You're right. I have very little idea about what has happened. Jill doesn't talk about her life as much."

"Take my word for it, Jill knows Leticia has stolen him," she answered dramatically. An arm draped across her anguished face would have been appropriate.

I ended the conversation with, "Maybe there's another side to the story," and left.

It wasn't until I left for the day that I saw Kelly. Most likely, because of Genevieve's earlier information, I was more aware of looking for him. Actually, I didn't realize I had seen him until I rounded Leticia's car to get to my own parked next to hers. As I tripped over the legs sticking outside the rear edge of Leticia's Mercedes, I spilled my briefcase and purse and then myself onto the parking lot, barely missing the back left fender of my own car with my head. Fortunately, my hands which broke the fall were the only damage suffered; my navy blue coatdress was unscathed. The torn hands would heal; a torn dress would not.

"Lady, what are you doing there?" Kelly asked gruffly. Not an "I'm sorry"; not a "Can I help you?"; not an "Are you hurt?" The least he could have done was help me up. I rose to a haunched position and tried to balance myself to gather my scattered possessions. Being too loaded with papers, books and general junk, both the small suitcase that is my purse and the larger suitcase that is my briefcase were too heavy to pick up. I carefully used by fingers to open a space in the straps to ease my forearms into the opening and try to pick them up. It was an exercise for a gold medal gymnast to try to heave myself up to a standing position while unable to use my palms to push myself up. Unfortunately, my five feet and ten inches prevented me from having the compactness of a gymnast, and my almost sixty years did nothing for my flexibility.

The longer this took, the more embarrassing the situation became and the angrier I got with the basketball player sized thug towering over me. When I had raised myself up, I looked at the chiseled face, into the brown eyes and parked the denigrating words I had intended to say at the back of my teeth.

He stood with both arms crossed, hands clenched into fists, eyes narrowed and teeth gritted. I am not a fearful woman, but I remembered my hurting hands and Leticia's marked face; I decided caution might be warranted.

"What were you doing under that car?"

"That's none of your business."

"That's Leticia's car."

"Score for you," he said sarcastically.

"Well?"

"Well, what?"

"What were you doing there?"

"I already told you, none of your business."

"Then, I'll go get Leticia to see if she knows."

"No!" he said quickly. We don't need to bother Leticia with this. Look, I'm sorry about your fall. Let me help you with those things." He reached out in an attempt to take my belongings, and I stepped out of his reach.

"So, what were you doing?"

"I, um, well, I noticed her muffler was a little loose. I wanted to see if I could, uh, you know, tighten it. Her car is too nice to get crapped up." He smiled, and the threat of him vanished. His body stance relaxed, his eyes widened and charm oozed over him like an oil slick on water. No wonder Leticia and Jill went weak in the knees for this joker.

"Sure," I agreed. "I have to clean my hands," I said and retraced my steps back to the office.

Genevieve was the only person I encountered when I went to the kitchen to disinfect my scraped hands.

"What happened?" she asked.

"I tripped over Leticia and Jill's boyfriend in the parking lot."

"Louisa," she said testily, "I've already told you about that. He is not Jill's boyfriend. Are you all right?"

"Sure, Genny, I can drive and write with my feet, no problem."

"Now, Louisa, this is no time for sarcasm. What do you need me to do?"

"I need you to wrap my hands with this gauze after I smear the antibiotic."

While bandaging, she was efficient both in her bedside manner and in extracting the details of my mishap. Maybe Gen should have been a nurse because she loves to be needed and be a part of life's emergencies.

She picked up my things, and, as she started to walk to my car with me, she started in, "I've told Jill to just leave him alone; just leave him alone. He's crass and rude and uncaring. Just leave him to Leticia; she thinks she can handle him. Just let her have him."

Just when I think I'm beginning to feel an affinity for Genny, she goes off on a rambling toot.

After the meeting yesterday, Leticia couldn't be found for most of the day. The next day, I managed to waylay her as I walked by her office. The good thing about being late most of the time is the ability to pull surprise maneuvers because no one knows when to expect me. Her raincoat and briefcase sitting in a side chair indicated her eminent departure.

I stepped inside the office and didn't say anything while she was kneeling and furiously rummaging through the bottom drawer of her desk. She was in such a hurry to escape the office, she still didn't see me standing at the door until she ran into me.

"Oh," she said.

"Hi," I said.

"Hi."

Out of curiosity I asked, "Is your boyfriend a mechanic?"

"What?" she was puzzled. "My boyfriend—a mechanic?"

"Yes. The one who was in the parking lot last night? He was fiddling with your car."

"You mean the big blond guy? Kelly? My *boy*friend!" she laughed.

"Does he work on your car?"

"Yeah, I guess so. He's a pretty good mechanic."

"Did you know he was doing something with your car last night?"

"Yeah, I guess maybe he said something about it."

"Well, did he or didn't he?"

"Louisa, you're so nosy. You're getting to sound a lot like Genevieve." She sneered her name.

"Okay, but did you tell him he could work on your car?"

"Yeah, okay, I did. Are you satisfied?"

"Yes. However, the real reason I came to talk to you is I thought you might want to finish what you had started the other night."

"What are you talking about?" Her annoyance should have warned me I was pushing my luck here.

"You do remember Monday night? You had me drive to your house with a problem you had. You said you needed my help."

"Monday night?"

"Yes."

"No, I don't remember anything."

"Leticia, what are you trying to pull? I was at your house Monday evening. You started to tell me something, and then the phone rang, and you sent me away."

"No, Louisa," she smiled with cool smugness. "None of you workers has ever been to my house."

I grabbed her arm. "Leticia, you're lying."

"Don't you ever touch me!" she said coldly as she yanked her arm from me, snatched her briefcase and coat, and strode out of her office.

Six

THESE CONDOMINIUMS HAD BEEN BUILT WITH A SPECIFIC market in mind. A blockbuster advertising campaign and high asking price had purchased their exclusivity that sold out the first phase before it was completed. As furiously as they climbed the corporate ladder, the young, upcoming professionals flocked to be the first buyers of the prestigious condo units. Gold-plated plumbing fixtures and solid wood moldings marked the units as the complex of the young nouveau riche, so one had only to mention his address and watch for the veiled envy in his listener's eyes. Each unit contained not one, but two master bedrooms. This was the gimmick the contractor had developed not only to make the homes appealing to this viable market, but also to make them affordable. How much easier it was to qualify for the exorbitant bankloan on two salaries than on one. Of course, some young professionals were married and didn't need to look for a flatmate able to share a bank loan and a lifestyle. This was the case in Unit Two in the Redwood Complex: here the residents were a married couple with a baby.

Mrs. Dilly in Unit Three was a tax break. Her young, professional son hadn't struggled up the corporate ladder; he walked up it with few impediments to block his way. Since his salary had risen with him, his accountant told him to buy a second house. As he was already the sole support of his mother, he installed her as his resident tax deduction. When first approached with his plan of having her live in his condo, she was concerned she wouldn't fit the lifestyle of the complex. Little did she understand that working one's way into upper-level management takes much energy making young professionals tired whey they get home at night. They don't have time to party; they can hardly

33

stoke up the energy to make it through the next workday. So, she led a quiet existence in her perfectly decorated piece of professional paradise.

Sometimes the couple next door had her baby sit. Sometimes they asked her to keep their baby for a weekend when they couldn't get him to daycare. He was a good baby. He never whimpered; he let anyone pick him up with no fuss. But he never smiled. He never cuddled, never babbled or cooed, and very seldom cried. Such a quiet, still little boy.

When Mrs. Dilly broke her hip, she didn't see the little guy for a few weeks. It had been a long stay in the hospital, so she thought maybe when she saw him again, he would have started talking. Her son had been very considerate to find such a pleasant convalescence at the senior home, and she had enjoyed it so much. There were people of her generation. Their history and hers intertwined, and reliving those histories made good conversation. As Mrs. Dilly's hip distress decreased, her homecoming ambivalence increased.

She arrived home on Thursday. She received the letter on Saturday. Taking the key that had been enclosed in the envelope, she pushed her walker to Unit Two. She opened the door and rushed to the second master bedroom. The smell of dirty diapers, old urine and sour milk assaulted her olfactories. Even in the wing of the convalescent home where non-ambulatory elders stayed, she had never been overpowered by smells of bodily functions as strong as these.

In the middle of the crib, on sheets stained by regurgitated milk and leaky diapers, he lay. Although he was longer and thinner, he was as quiet as she remembered him two months ago. In the room dimmed by drawn shades, she saw no recognition on his face.

"Oh, no, no, no. You shouldn't be here like this. No, no, this isn't right. No, no," she moaned.

She opened one of the three empty baby bottles by his side. The dregs smelled sour, and the milk in one bottle had congealed into a solid mass. She didn't call her son as she usu-

ally did when making a decision. She called the police. While she awaited their arrival, she took the baby in her arms and held him until she could no longer abide the smell of the filthy diaper. While she bathed him, the viciously red diaper area started to bleed out of the cracked skin. She cried; he didn't.

It was just as well she didn't have time to clean the nursery before the authorities swooped in. They needed to see for themselves the neglect the baby was suffering. Upon entering the home, the two policemen gagged. The state social worker plucked a tissue from her purse, held it over her nose and followed Mrs. Dilly's creaking walker to the nursery.

"Where are the parents, ma'am? Do you know?" the younger officer asked.

"I only got home on Thursday. They must have left him around then. A letter arrived today; it's in my condo next door. Just a scribbled note. This poor little baby," she said as ampules of tears collected at the base of her eyes.

As the social worker took pictures of the nursery, a police officer went to Mrs. Dilly's home to retrieve the letter. The remaining authorities gently probed Mrs. Dilly with questions to obtain as much background information as she could yield. Mrs. Dilly held the baby and tried to cuddle him. He didn't respond; he had never learned how. The social worker gathered the baby from the older woman's reluctant arms. She explained the baby would be placed in a foster home and probably become a ward of the court. Neglect charges would be brought against the parents, but until a judge heard the evidence, they would not know the final disposition of the child's case.

After all had left Unit Two in the Redwood Complex, Mrs. Dilly returned to her home. She called her son and plaintively requested to go back to the senior home.

Seven

I KNOW I PUT THE MUFFIN WAY BACK ON THE COUNTER; how Woofy reached it is beyond me. No muffin meant I couldn't have my lunch the American way—on the run with crumbs marking my path. My kids tell me I'm going to be late to my own funeral. Everyone's accepted that, except Charles. Too bad Woofy got sick on the carpet because it would have been easier to clean if he had thrown up on the tile. Then I wouldn't be so late. As I was thinking of any excuse other than dog nausea for my being late, I drove into the front parking lot of the agency. I might be able to sneak in without Charles' knowing it.

Dolly has always been helpful in fending Charles off for me, but she has never stood in the parking lot waiting for me. He must be extremely distressed because here she was wearing worry like a shroud.

"Louisa," she said as she ran to the car. "Oh, Louisa."

"Dolly, I can deal with Charles. I'm a good caseworker even if I am always late."

"Oh, no, Louisa. It's not that. It's…" and with that she started to cry. Her usually meticulously made-up, delicate face looked black and blue where mascara and eyeshadow had battled with tears.

"Leticia's dead! She's dead! She's in the file room, and she's dead!"

Dolly grabbed my arm to drag me inside the building to the hallway outside the file room. Under the leadership of Charles, logos, stationery and personnel had changed fairly quickly. Filekeeping, however, was changing fairly slowly. The goal had been to computerize all files within two years of Charles' arrival, but the agency had been around so long, and the files were so disheveled that it was going to be years before

Community Action Group entered the computer era of record management. We still had a huge room of high file cabinets. They were six drawers each about three feet across and sixteen inches high that made the overall height about ten feet. Because of the unwieldy height and the fact we live in earth-quake country, the cabinets were bolted to the studs of the walls. As a precaution, notices had been posted instructing us to close the drawers each time we used a cabinet. There had been accidents of people being hurt when the top drawer of a file cabinet was opened and tipped on the person while filing. Leticia, who is known for keeping stranger hours than most of us, must have worked late and filed papers.

Dolly half-pulled and half-shoved me through the crowd gathered in the hallway near the door of the fileroom. Like newly arrived troops at a battle, the police had commandeered the fileroom and its immediate surroundings, and it made jostling our way through police and medical workers difficult. Emotion and tears had so frustrated Dolly's garbled details of the story that she could only babble about Leticia's death.

Apparently, James, one of our Masters of Social Work trainees, had arrived first. Since he's so young and eager to be the best caseworker ever produced by a university, he had appointed himself caretaker of the office, turning on lights, computers and office machines, making coffee and picking up the mail at the post box. Because it was irregular to see lights on in the fileroom first thing in the morning, he had checked that room first after unlocking doors and saw an arm sticking out of the conglomeration of files, paper and fallen cabinet. He imme-diately called emergency.

By the time most of the staff were arriving for the day, the emergency crews had unearthed Leticia's body from the mounds of debris that had fallen on top of her. We got to the door just as Leticia was being taken out of the room by uni-formed personnel who could just as easily have been hotel waiters wheeling in a room service meal; they were so profes-sional about moving the cloth-covered gurney out. With just enough space in the open door to give us a peek, we could see one of the file cabinets lying on its side making a wall for a hillock of strewn files and papers. On the blank wall where the file cabinet had been lodged was a hole where a bolt had worked loose. Although two bolts per cabinet were suppose to have been installed, this one only had one bolt as it was so close to the door, and the studs were off line. The splash of linoleum not covered by papers must have been where Leticia fell and was crushed.

Rooted among the blue platoon of police was a tree of a guy, lanky limbs at his side, listening to one of the officers. I remembered him. His wife had introduced us a couple of times when she and I had worked together on some committees when our kids were in high school together. His shoulders stooped, but it made it seem that he listened all the more intently. His brown hair was a little sparser, and, from his pro- file, I could see he now wore glasses. His name was Sgt. Bob Washburn, but his wife had called him Bubba because he was her "country boy". I hadn't seen him for a couple years, not since her funeral.

Wanting information, I walked over to the group to say hello. The recognition was not immediate, but the intelligent eyes almost masked it as he scanned his memory for my name. While still searching he asked how I was and delivered the usual opening banalities.

"I haven't seen you since Lynn's funeral. How are you?"

"Now, I remember." He smiled apologetically, "I could be better. This isn't the best time to renew old acquaintances. I'm sorry it had to be this way."

"So am I. Do you know what happened?"

"Not really. First indications are an accident. See that bolt up there? It's worked loose. Looks like it might be on the edge of a stud and didn't quite catch the whole board. With the drawer opening and closing, it probably pulled loose over time."

He continued, "The woman must have left that top

drawer opened and then opened another drawer. That may have caused it to tip. I hope she was knocked out fast, so she didn't feel much."

"Sgt. Washburn, you mean she didn't die immediately?" I asked. "Oh, that's so terrible."

"I don't know, Mrs. Daniel." He had found my name. "I'm only supposing. I didn't mean to upset you."

Leticia never did follow the rules. She should have paid attention to the damn signs. I walked out of the room.

Thank heaven the paperwork I needed to complete was routine enough that it didn't require much concentration. It was a dreary day, made drearier by sadness and temerity on the faces of the staff. No one stayed late except those investigators who had a carte blanche to come and go as they needed.

Trying to recreate Leticia's last hours occupied my drive home. So many of us stay late at work to concentrate on jobs like writing reports or calling clients. But, why anyone would bother putting files back late at night when it could be done the next day was beyond me. Why waste your own time doing something like that? Most people are so exhausted at night, all they want to do is get home and relax. Wasting your own time on some menial chore compounded with the fact of being tired just added to my confusion. Most accidents occur because of being tired; perhaps that explained this one. Leticia was so tired, she didn't even think about the danger of leaving the top drawer open like that. If she suffocated, her death was a torturous process, and it made the idea of her dying even more difficult to absorb. What a horrible ending!

As I drove into the driveway at home, one good thought struck me. Sgt. Washburn still had those nice, kind eyes I remembered.

Eight

WHAT A WASTE! OF ALL THE DAYS TO BE LATE, I WASN'T ON Thursday. Emily hadn't called, and Woofy needed only a short walk, so I got to the office earlier than the other employees, even James. If I had been later, I might have missed some of the gloom that increased with the arrival of each person. By the middle of the day, the dreariness overwhelmed us. With each passing hour, stacks of files on the desks became higher because no one could go into the fileroom to put them away or retrieve new ones. The yellow plastic tape the police had placed on the door of the fileroom was made an insurmountable barricade by the dread of going into the room where Leticia had died. No one wanted to recall the death scene, neither did anyone want to risk another file cabinet unbolted from the wall and falling.

First thing in the morning, Charles had Dolly call a carpenter to check the bolts in the other cabinets. Second item was to make arrangements for Leticia's funeral which was difficult as there was not one emergency contact on any paper in her personnel folder. When approached about family members, Leticia always spat out, "It's none of your business. I take care of myself."

Later that morning, Kelly came in and spoke to Dolly. If there had been a director setting the scene, he could not have asked for better timing. As Leticia's boyfriend walked to Dolly's desk, Jill came from the back of the office. Indecipherable but strong emotions played tag across both faces. Seeing that, I went to see Genevieve, Madam Megabyte of office politics. She must know what was going on. Nobody could see their exchange in the waiting room and not realize Leticia's boyfriend and Jill had remnants of some kind of relationship.

41

Instead of finding Gen in my search, I ran into Charles in the hallway, and he requested my presence at an immediate emergency meeting in the conference room. He'd be there just as soon as he had requested the other staff members to appear. From past experience, we knew Charles' 'request' to be at a meeting left no option but to go, so we all dropped what we were doing and shuffled into the conference room.

Poor Charles! Even though the gold cuff links were perfectly placed on his red and white pin striped shirt, and the tan and red tie was perfectly knotted, and there was not one wrinkle in his camel colored suit, his clothing looked as crumpled as he did. Charles was so goal oriented that nothing would impede his fulfillment of whatever he set out to accomplish. To date, he had always found an acceptable solution to any problem confronting him. Not so, now. Leticia's death had caused him to lose a solid worker and had disrupted his organization. Perhaps he had even managed to be saddened by her demise, but he sure didn't like being sidetracked that way.

He opened with, "I'm sure we will all miss Leticia. She was a fine social worker and used many innovative ideas in achieving goals for her clients and the agency."

If any of us bothered to listen between the lines, we knew Charles was explaining how adept Leticia was at circumventing regulations. He probably would miss Leticia because most of the time she made the agency look good, but I couldn't believe he had a friendship with her that was any warmer than the rest of us had.

He continued with his eulogy, "We all know how she extended herself beyond her responsibility for each of her clients." This last statement exhibited Charles' tact. He never said one word about her effect on the staff. He concentrated only on her good quality.

"The police are finished in the fileroom with the investigation of the accident. We now have access to the room, so we can catch up on our cases. The carpenter has set up the fallen cabinet and reinforced the bolts on all the other cabinets as well.

"At my direction, Dolly has called the newspaper and the universities in the Bay Area to place ads in their employment classifieds. Until we have a very qualified social worker on board, I've taken Leticia's caseload and divided it among the rest of you. You'll each have about five extra cases temporarily."

He passed out the files on the new cases and closed the meeting. Each of us went to our offices to review our newly assigned charges. Nothing was heard, but faces indicated much mental grumbling at the extra work. Perusing the additions to my caseload, I found two of the people were at a nursing home I routinely visited. One was a child soon to be adopted. One was a young toddler considered unadoptable. The last one was, and this was a pleasant surprise, Mrs. Streng. Charles, in consideration, had balanced the caseload, so it would not create a terrible hardship to my current caseload.

On the way out of the office that evening, Dolly said, "Leticia's funeral is taken care of. Charles had her sent to the funeral home."

"You found some family?" I asked.

"No. We didn't even know where to begin. Every official document we checked had the same sketchy information we already had."

"So, who's paying for the funeral?" I knew we didn't collect enough when the hat was passed.

"Jill and Leticia's boyfriend," she answered.

That was a surprise. "Kelly? Why would he do that?"

"I don't know. He said it didn't seem right to send her off without some fanfare."

"He's either a nicer person than he appears, or…"

"Or what?" Dolly asked.

"Nothing, I guess. I'm not sure what I was going to say."

"Well, after all the trouble he's caused, he should feel really guilty. Poor Jill is so confused." Dolly had closed the office down for the evening, so we walked out together.

Approaching the parking lot, I asked, "Why do you say that? Has Jill said anything to you?"

"Not in so many words. After the police left though, I stepped into the restroom, and she was in there crying. I asked if I could help and she said no. But then she said something very peculiar."

"Which was?"

"You know how people are when they cry. Everything rockets around your head, and even if you understand it, it sounds as though you've forgotten how to talk, so nobody else understands what you understand."

"So, what did she say?"

"Something like 'Kelly feels' or 'Kelly is bad', something like that."

"Kelly again. Guess I need to find out more about this guy."

"As much as we talk about him, you'd think you'd know everything we know. You need to come and eat lunch with us. Even Charles doesn't expect you to work during your lunch hour. You work too hard. Besides, if you ate with us, you'd find out all kinds of juicy information,"

"That's probably true," I said sarcastically. "Genny never misses a lunch."

"You got that right. Bye"

Putting my key in the doorlock of my car, I happened to look to the end of the parking lot and saw Kelly opening the door on the driver's side of Leticia's car. At least, it appeared it was he. There was another person in the car. From that distance, it looked like Jill.

After Woofy's walk, I started to examine more closely the case files inherited from Leticia I had brought home. Charles didn't like confidential records going out of the office, but because time was at a premium in keeping continuity for these people, I made a management decision and decided their needs were more important than his rules. As expected, Leticia, with her usual scrupulous recordkeeping, had excellent information. The little unadoptable toddler and Mrs. Streng would take the most time; the others were more a matter of overseeing the people taking care of them. In Mrs. Streng's carefully kept file were many notes and paper that meant it wouldn't be hard to pick up where Leticia had been interrupted.

Deciding I would visit these people Monday, I closed the files, but as I started to put them into my briefcase, several papers that appeared to be invoices from Mrs. Streng's folder fell to the floor. As it required some minutes to pick them up, I put them in chronological order and carefully clipped them inside the file. That done, I got ready for bed, made like I was settling in for a long read with a good book and promptly and soundly fell asleep.

Nine

THE WEEKEND WAS RAINY AND MERCIFULLY QUIET. There were no social gatherings at my daughter's house to attend. The child is over thirty and still feels guilty if she doesn't share blame, somehow, for my divorce and the loneliness it sometimes creates. In her constant searching out the perfect companion for me, she exorcises some kind of grief and atones for something which wasn't her fault. No mating calls to attend enabled me to do housework at a leisurely pace. Far from drudgery, I found this relaxing because I seldom had time to do it, and it provided a nice break in the routine of my job. All that cleaning made me feel organized and ready to warp speed through my deskwork the next week.

The weekend rain made Monday as clear and bright as my newly cleaned house. Some people are intrigued; others are exasperated by the idea of California running against the grain of the rest of the country. Even the weather displays this proclivity. In the winter it rains; in the summer it doesn't. As a result, the hills of California are warm, dried gold in the summer and cool, yellow green velour in the winter. When it stops raining, it stops raining. There's really no warning like a few drippy days to proclaim the rain coming to an end. One week it is wet enough for Noah and his ark; the next week it will be dry enough for Lawrence and his camels. Once the rain stops, the complete color transformation of the hills takes only two to three weeks, as quickly as changing the tint button of a television.

Driving is one of the highlights of my job. It gives a freedom that many jobs don't have. When one situation becomes too intense, I can leave it to go to another more inviting environment and, while driving, contemplate the day and its happenings. Driving through the hills is one of the best excursions because the stillness of the surroundings lends itself to reflection. Since the hills are protected from the California building frenzy by lying on an earthquake fault zone, the grazing cows are the few living, breathing bodies around. This means little traffic, congestion and confusion. To get to Mrs. Streng's house, I had to drive through the countryside. I thought Leticia's home had been the height of exclusivity, but seeing Mrs. Streng's house made me realize I should have reserved judgment. Her home was so exclusive, there wasn't another building within ten acres of it.

Before Contra Costa cultivated its suburbs and bedroom communities, it cultivated walnuts, tomatoes, beef, pears, and mutton. The ranch and farms that raised these products were usually divisions of old Spanish land grants given to people by the rulers of Spain in the 1600's. Any of the remaining haciendas on the original grants are now historical monuments; however, some of the later ranch houses on the divided parcels are still used as residences. Mrs. Streng's house was obviously one of these. Although tasteful additions had been added as the needs of the generations living in the house changed, the original part of the house, which was the main living area, retained much of the natural wood and Spanish design used in the early 1800's. Enough land had been kept, so the house did not dwarf its setting. Fragrant eucalyptus, probably from the original batch brought from Australia; California oaks; and a few redwoods and deodora pines defended the house from the view of any interloper who might presume to drive the distance up the narrow driveway to Mrs. Streng's.

The son I had seen at the agency last week answered the door. Although he was older than I remembered him at first sighting, he obviously had access to a gym. His iridescent blond hair, aqua blue eyes, and light sifting of freckles across the bridge of his nose decreased his age even more. The only things lacking to complete his all-American boy image were a cowlick and a lopsided grin on his face.

"Hello," I introduced myself, "I'm Louisa Daniel, a social worker from the agency your mother has been using. Leticia Gallegos, who had been working with your mother, had a shocking accident and won't be able to provide her usual services.

"Mr. Overton, the director of the agency, I think you know him, has assigned Mrs. Streng's case to me. Dolly was going to call you about all this, but she was unable to get through to you. She said she left a message on your answering machine. Did you receive it?"

"Yes, Mrs. Daniel, I did. We're glad you're here. Actually, Mr. Overton did call and explain the circumstance. Your agency and Leticia's family have my family's deepest condolence. Juggling and rescheduling is tough on all office members, but losing a family member's life must be even harder on Leticia's family," he said graciously.

"My name is Percival Hough-Streng. Come in and meet mother. She appears a bit down today. I told her about Leticia, but I'm never sure how much she comprehends. I'm afraid Zoë won't be here today. She's my sister. She knew you were coming and very much wanted to meet you. She and I share the responsibility of mother's care. Frankly, I don't think either of us could do this by ourselves. Periodically we have a nurse come in to help us out.

"Mother has aphasia, you know. She can't talk to us, and we have no way of carrying on conversation. She had always been such a good conversationalist before her accident, so witty and articulate. Until she got sick, I never realized the importance of sending and receiving information via talking. This is a situation that doesn't create much depth in relationships. Her speech therapist tried to get her to use a communication board, but it was unsuccessful. Mother didn't seem to respond to that therapist."

As Mr. Hough-Streng explained all this, we walked into a magnificent living room furnished with European wall tapestries, antiques, and not of the old oak icebox genre either. These

were British Queen Anne and French Louis XIV pieces pep-
pered with a few good old American Duncan Phyfe units.
Because the heavy colors in the tapestries and the natural wood
ceilings and walls made the room dark, the array of beveled
glass French doors along the back wall of the house and the
white patterned area rugs sparked the room to pleasing light-
ness. That was my visual pleasure for the day. Persian carpets
guided our walk down the hallway lined with photographs and
portraits of a long line of Strengs and Houghs and other family
members. Dour, dark clothed reproduction of tintypes from the
late 1800's and early twentieth century started our trek down
the hall. Our parade down the visual timeline carried us past
carefree, bejeweled flappers and high-collared young men of
the twenties. By the time we reached the thirties, I began recognizing some family members. There was a very young vision
of Mrs. Streng, innocent and guileless, and as beautiful as when
she was older. Brothers and sisters, or perhaps cousins, surrounded her. Mr. Streng, stern and massive, emerged, and there
was baby Percival and then toddler Percival and then youthful
Percival looking very much like his father. By the late fifties, a
smaller, dark-haired man was seated next to Mrs. Streng. There
nestled among Percival and his parents was a fourth family
member, who I took to be the sister I had not yet met. The single portrait of her could have been a twin of the single portrait
of Mrs. Streng taken in the thirties. Time continued on in the
pictures of brother and sister, parents and children, aunts and
uncles, reunions of relatives, shirt tail and otherwise. When we
reached the end of memory lane, we still hadn't completed the
stretch of the hallway. I had been intrigued enough with the
family portraits that we hadn't said much but then picked up
the discussion Percival Hough-Streng had started.

"Excuse me, just what is a communication board?"

"Ours is very simple. I understand they can be quite
complex and use computers. The computer use is for people
permanently limited in communication like the cerebral
palsied, brain-damaged, paralyzed, those types of limitations.

Ours is a poster with pictures such as a bowl of food, a toilet, a bed, clothes, all the items necessary for Mother's comfort. Then, with her functioning arm, she can point to the objects as she needs them," he said.

Just as he finished that last statement, we walked into what was obviously a garden room. Although the bedclothes coordinated with the delft blue and white fabric on the upholstery, the hospital bed was incongruous in the middle of the lush greenery that surrounded the white wrought iron furniture. The bed was placed so it looked out the wall of French doors and floor to ceiling windows onto a verdant park topped by the three pronged Mt. Diablo in the distance. In the foreground was Mrs. Streng's estate. Masses of roses, aromatic gardenias and pendulous, purple plumes of wisteria punctuated the green mat of blue grass.

"Oh! What a beautiful setting. This would be sure to cheer any convalescence."

"Thank you, it is lovely, isn't it? I decided to put Mother here thinking the same thing," he said with a slight emphasis on the "I". "The poor old thing can't walk back to her own room, and we can't very well leave her in the living areas for guests to trip over."

"No, I suppose not," I said walking around to the foot of the bed. Sadly, this woman did not much resemble the Mrs. Streng with whom I was familiar. The acrid pungency of Mrs. Streng was pitiable, but in spite of the stained blue robe and the matted, greasy hair, she had managed to maintain some grace. The facial paralysis, which can be the result of brain trauma gave her a harlequin's face. One side drooped into a lifeless frown; one side seemed to slightly smile as she looked at me.

"Hello, my name is Louisa Daniel," I introduced myself since her son didn't seem inclined to do so. "I'm a social worker with the same agency where Leticia Gallegos worked. We've met before at some agency functions and board meetings. Leticia had a terrible accident and won't be able to see her clients anymore, so I'm taking her place."

At the mention of Leticia, the barely perceptible smile dropped.

"Mother," Mr. Hough-Streng almost shouted, "this is Louisa Daniel. She will be taking over Louisa's job. Louisa had an accident."

Puzzled at his repetition of my introduction, I looked at Mrs. Streng to see a glazed, expressionless façade overtake her face. Mrs. Streng started nodding off. Percival took my elbow and escorted me out of her room and down the memory-laden hallway. While walking to the door, he explained his mother's doctor had told him an enhanced stimulus might help in over-coming some of her inability to communicate. As a result, he always spoke to her loudly. He shunted me out the house with a courtly but abrupt good-bye and shut the door.

Ten

M<small>Y NEXT STOP TO VISIT NEW CLIENTS WAS A CALL TO</small> the unadoptable toddler. Sometimes the agency would take on clients who were lost in bureaucratic cracks, those cases the county or state governments in their net of red tape couldn't get a line on. The hope was that they would eventually be placed in foster homes, senior hospices or battered women shelters, but, until the necessary legalities were satisfied, we provided temporary respite care for them. This was another coup for Charles who recognized a community need we could fill and make good use of tax dollars in doing so. To get these people situated, Charles had several boarding homes with which our agency dealt. People were placed in these clean and safe environments. Oftentimes they were so traumatized by a personal disaster, this was the only haven they had had in weeks or months.

The facility to which I headed was just such a place for babies and young children. Mrs. Chu, the owner of the home, was a widow who enjoyed working with children, so as her own kids went their own ways, she decided to repopulate her domicile with other kids. When her home was accepted by the agency and passed by the state licensing board, she moved out half of her furniture and equipped almost every room as a nursery. She was allowed four children at a time, and because she provided such excellent care, she was always at maximum capacity. Almost inevitably, when the time came to place a child in a permanent situation, Mrs. Chu suffered terrible heartache because she attached herself to each child like a mama opossum.

"Mrs. Daniel" her attempt at a smile was cut off by a sneeze as she answered the door, "I haven't seen you for months. Dolly said you were coming. Little Ian is one of my favorites."

"They're all your favorites," I answered rummaging though my purse for the notes I had made. "Ian? That's not his name, is it? I don't think that's in my notes."

"His name is Ian," she said.

So be it. Mrs. Chu had no compunction about renaming her charges if they appeared to her to be in need of renaming. Maybe by giving them new names, she felt they could have a new, better start in their lives.

"Come see him. He's a pity."

The baby was about fifteen months old, yet he did not sit in the playpen. Looking up at the ceiling, he didn't turn his head as we walked up to him. I reached to pick him up, but he didn't smile. He lay still and nonresponsive. I called his name, both of them, but he didn't turn his head to face me. His passivity had become his defense.

Mrs. Chu didn't just provide physical necessities for these kids which was one of the reasons she was such a gem in caretakers. She read constantly to them; she had them grouped around her playing games, talking, and watching wholesome children's shows. She would do the same with Ian—anything to give this forlorn, handsome, blue-eyed baby a positive pat in his world of negative nurturing. In the hour or so with them, I held Ian, but there was no response. He was like the rhesus monkeys everyone in Psych 101 learned about. One group of monkeys had been held and given affection; one group hadn't. The cuddled group thrived; the neglected group died.

My goals for the day accomplished, I set out for home. The gas gauge on the dash was riding on 'e' as in desperate, so I hustled over to a gas station, thinking of Ian and Mrs. Streng the whole ride. Two worlds apart, both in ages and in circumstances, but so similar in ability, or lack of it, to fulfill their needs. Neither one could communicate which meant having to rely on others to provide for their needs but never having any relationships and always being alone.

I hadn't quite warp sped through my desk the day before as planned, so that was my intention to do so today. But, when I got to the office, Dolly had put an urgent call note from Mrs. Chu on my desk. I returned the call and realized her sneeze of yesterday had become a cold today. Therefore, she asked in her muffled voice if I would please take Ian for a few days. She had found safe places for all her other babies to keep them from contagion, but she didn't want to put Ian with anyone new. She felt that having him to get to know someone else would delay getting responses from him.

"Could you please, Mrs. Daniel, take him? It would only be a few days. Please? He needs consistency in his life to so much."

Soft touch and bleeding heart, especially for kids and dogs. Of course, I said, "No problem. I'll be out today to get him. Pack some things, and I'll locate a crib."

She was nicely appreciative, but as I rearranged the day, the big issue became not how I was to clean up the paperwork of last week but where I would find a crib. Sure, no problem. It also meant Ian was going to be my companion on rounds.

Emily hadn't called today, so it seemed circumstances warranted my calling her.

"Emily," I said as she answered, "it's your mother."

"I know, Mom. What do you need?"

She was always a perceptive child.

"A crib."

"You mean for a baby?"

"Yes."

"Congratulations, but aren't you a little old to be having children?"

"I'm babysitting. There's an emergency at work."

"Ah," she said knowingly. "This is a child who has no home, no parents, no love, no clothes, no anything. Am I close?"

"On the nose. Do you have a crib?"

"No, my dear, dear mother," she chuckled, "but for you, I

will scrounge and find one. Give me a few hours and then come for dinner. I'll have it. And, Mom?"

"Yes?"

"Bring your friend."

"My friend?"

"The little child."

"Bye, love, and thanks."

Maybe after she met him, she would offer to take him some of the time while I worked.

As well kept as Leticia's files had been, it wouldn't hurt to get some information from Mrs. Streng's physician. I called her office and was told she would have time that day at 11:45 to brief me. For the second time that day, I mentally rearranged my schedule to beat it over there.

Passing by the file room, I saw James handing files to Dolly on the stool to put in the upper drawers. When the file cabinet was righted, the workmen had piled the fallen files to one side of the room. Each of us was asked to take an hour of our nonexistent spare time to file. Although we all tried to comply, Dolly and James would probably end up doing most of the refiling. What a job!

Find the missing item in this picture. As it struck me, I stopped, put myself in reverse and asked them," Did you get a new stool?"

"A new stool?" asked James.

"Right. Wasn't the other one crushed?"

"No, why would we want a new stool?" Dolly asked this time.

"You didn't get a new one?" I asked again.

"Louisa, we just told you—no," they both said in unison.

Leaving it at that I told them, "No reason," and left for Dr. Cannaughton's office.

That was puzzling though. The police said Leticia was filing and must have pulled the drawer open which would give the final tug to unbolt the cabinet from the wall. If that were the case, she would have had to use the stool to get to the top drawer. And, if she had to use the stool, it should have been crushed as she was. It wasn't, and that was strange.

Eleven

A TWENTY MINUTE WAIT INDICATED THAT DR. Canaughton really didn't have time to see me. After meeting her and telling what information I was after, she said, "My field is internal medicine, but, over the years, I've developed an interest in gerontology, which is the care of elders. When my nurse told me about your call, I wanted to meet you for two reasons. One is the need for someone to understand what is happening to Mrs. Streng; the other is to pontificate a bit." She smiled.

"When I think about Mrs. Streng, I wonder why she didn't get to us earlier. Do you know much about strokes?"

Seeing me nod negatively, she started in, "There are basically two kinds of strokes or cerebral vascular accidents—CVA's we call them. One is a blockage type where a blob of blood or fat will block blood from passing through a vein. Usually the veins are narrowed by plaque. Those account for about seventy five to eighty percent of all strokes. The other kind, like Mrs. Streng had, is a bleeding type and accounts for about twenty percent of strokes. An artery with weakened walls will balloon out and burst. There might be some variations of these, but that's basically what happens in a stroke.

"Now, what's interesting about all this, and this is why I like to get on the soapbox, is that not many people are aware of strokes. They know about heart attacks; they don't know about strokes. Yet strokes affect almost as many people as heart attacks. The preventions are the same, too. Lowering blood pressure is extremely effective, quitting smoking, watching cholesterol—all those that work for high-risk people in the heart attack area work for high-risk in the stroke area."

She went on, "I'll tell you something else interesting about strokes. People with heart attacks usually have only minutes to live. People with CVA's are usually warned in advance. Things like chronic, abnormal headaches, weakness in a limb, speech difficulties like slurring words, dizziness or falling, dimming vision—all these can be warnings.

"I don't know if Mrs. Streng had any of these, but I bet a dime to a doughnut she did. She may have passed it off as flu or a tension headache. Oftentimes, when people come to us with those problems, we can run tests and start them on anticoagulants and have pretty good success. Some people started on these preventions early enough in the stroke may show no residual effects of the stroke.

"I must apologize. I know I'm taking time, but I feel so few people know about this, and it's important to me that I educate any captive audience. Besides, it's good background for you to understand Mrs. Streng. Did you know Mrs. Streng before the accident?"

"Yes, but in a professional capacity. She sits on our agency's board, so our dealings have always been on a business basis. Even if she didn't know me well personally, she was always as gracious and helpful as if I were a good friend."

Dr. Cannaughton nodded as she said, "There are some other things. She was an active person. She swam; she played tennis; she walked. Usually stroke victims who are active like that recover a little more quickly than others. I've talked with her speech therapists, and they see very little oral speech. They have no feel for her receptive language—what she understands. Occupational and physical therapists haven't seen much progress either.

"We've set her up for tests. Sometimes she gets there; sometimes she doesn't. The family feels she tires so easily, and she has bad days, so they either cancel or don't show. I just wish there were more I could do to help her. It seems a shame to have that vibrancy lost."

"That's true," I agreed. "Her former caseworker would

take her to some of the appointments her kids couldn't get her to. I'll do anything like that when I can."

There was a pause, and as I started to walk to the door, Dr. Cannaughton said, "You know, the kids are very concerned about her. They're so attentive when one of them brings her in here. I hope it pays off for her recovery."

"So do I. You've been very kind in giving up your lunch. I didn't intend to disrupt your schedule, but I appreciate your taking your time to help Mrs. Streng,"

"Glad to do it. Thanks for letting me ramble. Maybe it will help some of your other clients," she said as she walked with me out of the room.

One more stop. Locating Sgt. Washburn at City Hall was as tough as finding a dropped contact lens on a city sidewalk at quitting time. There were no faces to speak with; there were only stacks of paper with legs rushing away from me. It wasn't until a clerk told me that I was looking for Lieutenant Washburn instead of Sergeant Washburn that I realized what had created my difficulty in finding him. When we finally did connect, my frazzle matched his. His face was harried with the dealings of the day, but his nice eyes smiled when he saw me.

"Hello, Mrs. Daniel. My name is Bob. Do you mind if I call you Louisa? My office is down here."

"Yes, I prefer Louisa. I'm sorry to bother you, but you were at the scene of Leticia's accident, and I'm not sure this is important, but I thought I'd come to you. Maybe you wouldn't be interested, but I found it peculiar." I wasn't organizing my presentation too well, but by then, we had arrived at his office.

Looking around as he shut the door, I hoped the promotion carried some other benefits with it because it sure wasn't in his office. Besides the obligatory stacks of files any busy person has on the desk, floor and file cabinets, there was an electric typewriter, a very old computer, an olive chair with stuffing peeking out the seams and several different colored layers of institutional paint evidenced by scrapes on the walls. He did have a window. At least, he wouldn't have to look at that ratty décor because he could look out onto the police cars in the parking lot.

"Look, Lt. Washburn, Bob. Leticia should have been on a stool in that room. If the upper drawer were open, she couldn't file unless she had something to stand on. None of us can reach the higher drawers. Well, some can reach them, but none of us can actually get into them to work."

I continued. "There was no crushed stool. If she went into the file room to put away or take out records, she would have dragged the stool over to the cabinet, stood on it and pulled the drawer. Then, if the cabinet fell, the stool should have been crushed, too.

"There was no crushed stool. As I left the office today, it hit me. James and Dolly were filing those spilled cases from the accident. She was on the stool, but it was the old stool. It wasn't even bent like it seems it should have been if it had a heavy object fall on it."

No reaction from him to this, so I rephrased my conclusion, "There is no new stool because the old one which should be smashed didn't need replacement."

He still didn't react, so with greater emphasis, I said, "If Leticia had been filing, she would have been on the stool."

He seemed to mentally measure what I was saying. "Let me see. You are here about the Gallegos case. You found something unusual, and you have made the quantum leap from accident to what? Murder?"

"I don't know. I really don't. There are many people who aren't fond of Leticia, but she never hurt anyone, I don't think. She could be extremely aggravating, but that's a big assumption."

Now irony poked at the edges of his eyes. "Right. It is a big step. Think about it some more. I will, too. But you know about 'ifs', and there are many 'ifs' in what you just told me."

At least he didn't flick the idea away like a pesky gnat.

After a pause, he said, "Sometimes when there is an accident, especially a freak accident, people have a need to find a reason. It doesn't make sense that someone didn't cause it. I think that's why there are so many lawsuits. People want a someone to blame, not a something."

He continued to neuter my embarrassment, "Your reaction is not unusual. An accident like that is a terrific shock. It's okay. It's not even hard to see how you could come up with that."

Someone passed by the door, gave him a nod to which he said, "I'll be right there." I stood up when he did, and we walked out. As I left him, I shook his hand good-bye.

It must have been my disorganized state that made me think he held my hand a bit longer than necessary.

Twelve

WHEN CHARLES COMPLETED THE STANDARD announcements and reminders about the Jail-Bail at the staff meeting, he said he had one more sensitive issue to take up.

He began with, "I don't usually interfere with our employee's personal lives. However, there is a predicament occurring that I want to handle in the best possible manner, causing the least amount of notice to the people involved. I know there is a gentleman connected with Leticia loitering around the parking lot."

Everyone turned to gaze at Jill who put her head in her hands and liquefied into her chair.

Charles continued, "If this young man is bothersome to any of you, I want you to know I'll obtain a restraining order against him and prevent him from coming onto the property. Please see me later if any of you wish to have this done."

Genevieve's nasal, sing-song voice heralded her presence near my office. Her whine was mellowed by Jill's soft monosyllables. The duet stopped at my door and entered with clipboards in their hands.

"Louisa, you really must sign up for your duty at the Jail-Bail," Gen began a harangue. "Charles has passed this clipboard around two weeks now, and several of you haven't signed up. Jill and I volunteered to fill the missing spots to help out poor, busy Charles. We can't shirk our duties, can we, dear? This is for a wonderful cause. We have several jobs here. I came to you first because I know you want to be sure to fulfill your obligation. I've decided you could probably do one or two of these pretty well, so I've taken the liberty of putting your name by the ones I think you could handle."

Turning to Jill, she affirmed, "You know what good friends Louisa and I have been in the past. She knows I can read her like a book, so I just assigned her to a duty. She'll do a wonderful job.

"Louisa, you couldn't be auctioneer because a man has to do that one. Your voice just wouldn't be loud enough. You couldn't be jailer because you might lose the keys. You know how you're always losing your car keys. You couldn't be greeter; you're never on time."

While she carried on the about the joys of our friendship and the litany of my shortcomings, I took the clipboard and signed up to be banker. Gen hadn't put my name anywhere near that job. It was a two-hour shift, and I could probably count money to someone's satisfaction, although not Genevieve's. I also wrote a check to purchase my obligatory tickets, figuring I could give them to Emily and David who would use them or give them away to friends or business buddies. They like those social fundraisers, and they'll know half the people there.

In the twenty years that I've known Genevieve, I have learned to ignore most of her backhanded compliments and underhanded jibes. Every once in awhile, however, she'll get me. It's usually when I'm tired, thinking hard, or discouraged. Today she did it. She loved it so much I could almost see the mental tick of a point for her when I said, "I don't lose my keys anymore. I have two sets now, and I carry one set in my purse and one in my pocket."

She looked down smiling broadly and said, "Banker? Oh dear. No, I don't think you could do that. I had you in mind for clean up or kitchen duty. You know how you don't like to go to those big gatherings. If you did what I chose for you, you wouldn't have to get dressed in one of those shabby old dresses of yours. I really think you should rethink the job you chose."

She was going for another zinger, but, this time, I had the stamina to parry her verbal thrust.

"That's it, Gen. It's either that or nothing. I'll buy some

more tickets and not go and fill my obligation that way, but you know Charles wants all the agency's staff there. He told us we were to purchase extra tickets only if we had an extreme emergency and couldn't be there. If I tell him I'm not going because you didn't think I should have that job, he won't be happy."

Jill said with an amused and reassuring smile, "It's fine, Louisa. Genny and I appreciate your willingness to help, don't we, Gen?"

"Well, I don't know. I just don't know," Genevieve said as Jill steered her out the door to corral another staffer.

There were a couple of counseling sessions to conduct in the office. Emily said she'd have the crib late this afternoon. If I timed it right, I could pick up Ian, see Mrs. Streng since she's out that way and get to Emily's without having to come back to the office.

Standing in the fileroom with the intent of putting away the two cases I had just seen, I started wondering again why Leticia would be in this room that night. The police seemed to think she had been working late into the night. Although most of us will stay a couple hours after closing, I could not ever remember anyone staying that late. Part of the reason for that is the agency is not in the most secure area of Pleasant Creek. We've never had any trouble, but there are security grids on the window. Charles and the board have been extremely conscientious in keeping us apprised of safety measures and precautions.

It might be wise to look at the files Leticia was working on to see if there was anything unusual in any of them. The other caseworkers who were given the remainder of her caseload would let me check these files, so I put that on my list of activities for the week. Seeing Gen and Jill in the hallway, each with a stack of files to be put away, I followed them back to the fileroom. Before Gen could start on her tirade about my Jail-Bail job, I asked, "Does either of you know why Leticia was here so late the night she had her accident?"

Jill frowned as Gen started in, "Well, dear. I think she had something wrong with her car, the brakes or something. It was in the shop. I asked her that evening when I left if she wanted a ride, but you know how curt she was. She told me to just leave her alone. *She* could get along just fine. *She* didn't need any help. And, *she* certainly didn't want *my* help.

"So I left. I never did ask how she planned to get home. She was the hardest woman to talk to. I never could believe her clients liked her as much as Charles claimed they did. I mean, she was never nice to me. How could she be nice to them? Of course, some of it may have been that she knew she couldn't pull the wool over my eyes. I could read her like a book. She just avoided me because she knew I couldn't be manipulated like the rest of you. Not you, of course, Jill. You're too perceptive. I always tried to include her in our conversations. She just looked down her nose at me."

Taking a deep breath, she continued, "I used to talk to her about that boyfriend. I used to tell her he was no good. Just like I tell Jill how lucky she is not to be around him now. Isn't that right, Jill?"

Jill did a fish gape when she started to open her mouth to say something. Genevieve doggedly trudged on in her diatribe against Kelly.

"If these younger girls would listen to us, they could learn a lot from our situations, isn't that right, Louisa? Why should they have to suffer the heartaches our husbands put us through? I mean, after all, they could learn from our mistakes."

Her pink, this week, beehive hairdo quivered as she orated on the shortcomings of men.

"Men just don't turn out like we think they're going to, do they, Louisa? You know, that first husband of mine was so mean. He was always telling me I talked too much. I told him he just needed to listen to me, but he said he didn't like to listen to me because he never thought I said anything worthwhile. I told him how I was just trying to help him, and he could really use my help in some of these problem areas. I mean, after all, I was trained to help people and their quirks. That's my profession.

"Now, my Sid. He's wonderful. Never says a mean word to me. That's what you need, both of you. Someone who sits with his beer and smiles all the time. He listens to me. He's a treasure."

Simultaneously, Jill and I gave up and left Gen standing talking to the wall for a few moments before she realized we had left.

Leticia's last night sidled up to my thoughts as I drove to get Ian. If her car were in the shop, and she appeared unconcerned about needing a ride somewhere, then what? Was she planning to get a bus or taxi? Though why should she if someone had offered her a ride? Even if it were someone whom she was not fond of, going home with Gen would be better than having to pay for transportation. On the other hand, it seemed more likely she was to meet someone. But who would it be at that time? A co-worker? That was doubtful. If it were a private matter, wouldn't they just stay past the time when everyone else had left? Or better yet, they could meet somewhere where no one would recognize them. Besides, there weren't any employees who like Leticia enough to want to stay with her. Maybe she was going to meet her boyfriend. Or maybe a client. In that case, Dolly should have a record in the appointment or logbooks.

Mrs. Chu had a car seat she let me use for the little boy. She had gathered a few toys, bottles, clothes, and other baby accessories in a large box, and she had even packed a diaper bag. I hoped caring for babies is like riding a bicycle: one never loses the ability even though it hasn't been used for awhile. The little fellow looked uncertain when he came to me, but he held onto my neck with his little hand. In between sniffles and sneezes, Mrs. Chu told me he had started to smile a little at the other children but still didn't play with the toys they left lying around. She said he was sitting on his own and gazing for long periods of time at different objects, but he still didn't talk or make noises. He'd also put on a pound, so he was eating well enough.

In the car, I started talking to him. I talked about the cows on the hills, the colors we were seeing, and anything else I thought an almost two year old would be interested in. When I ran out of preschool subjects, I started talking about Mrs. Streng. To her house was where we were going next.

Talking to Ian was like talking to Woofy—a completely one-sided conversation.

Thirteen

I PULLED THE CAR AS CLOSELY TO THE DOOR OF MRS. Steng's manor as I could, parked under a tree, so Ian wouldn't get hot, and I could see him, and rolled down the windows. Going up to the door, I rang it, watching the car and Ian while I did so. The woman who answered the door was a younger version of Mrs. Streng, just as regal and gracious.

On introducing myself, she said, "My name is Zoë Streng. I was hoping to meet you. Percival told me about Leticia's accident and all that has happened. I was very sad to hear it because the few times I had seen her with Mother seemed very productive. Mother appeared to respond to her quite nicely. It almost seemed like we could see her beginning to heal.

"I'm sorry I missed you earlier, but I work outside the home, and I have to schedule around that. I keep hoping each time I return from work, I'll see more improvement in Mother. It just seems like she should be healing."

I agreed. "Apparently, her doctor feels the same way. I spoke with her and got the idea she expected a quicker recovery for Mrs. Streng."

"Come back and see her," she invited.

"Before we do…" I interrupted. "I have a baby in the car, and I'd like to bring him in. Would you mind? It's not normally done, but the boarding home mother is ill, and she requested I keep him. She feels a familiar face would be easier for him."

"Percival's not here, but Mother and I love babies. Please bring him to see her; it might be just the lift she needs."

With Ian in my arms, we greeted a Mrs. Streng pleasantly different from when I had first seen her at her home. Zoë had attempted to resurrect the former Mrs. Streng and had almost succeeded. Her hair was coifed; her dirty, blue robe was replaced by black silk loungewear trimmed in flat gold braid. She had on light make up, and the diamond rings she habitually wore before her stroke flashed on her hands. Except for the immobile half-face, one would not realize she was convalescing. Upon seeing the baby, she reached for the communication board, but it fell to the floor with a clatter. I started to walk across the room to retrieve it for her, but her daughter placed her hand on my arm and quietly said, "Let her go; she needs to get it for herself."

With some effort, Mrs. Streng picked it up, smiled slightly at her victory and pointed to the letters, 'b' and 'a'. Miss Hough-Streng said, "She'd like to hold the baby. Is it all right?"

As I placed Ian in her good arm, I said, "Mrs. Streng, I'm happy to see you more like your old self. It's like meeting a friend."

She looked at me briefly, but her attention was occupied by Ian who also attracted Zoë's attention until she remembered me in the corner.

"I'm sorry, Mrs. Daniel," she said. "I forgot my manners. He is so sweet. Can you tell me his story?"

I told her as much as I was legally able. Her eyes teared when she heard how he was found. She went to her mother, took Ian, and held him while I continued the story.

"Do you think he will be adopted?" she asked.

"It's doubtful. Even if the parents relinquish their rights, most families want to adopt young babies. They want to start fresh, and a toddler is hardly a fresh start. Besides Ian has already lived a hard life, and it's difficult to predict the effect on his learning, intelligence, and even physical growth."

As we discussed Ian, Percival charged into the room. The all-American boy was agitated and reddened with emotion.

"What's going on?" he said obviously trying to keep his responses in check. "Zoë, I've told you Mother cannot be allowed to become overly excited. You should know better than to bring a baby in here. This could kill her."

While Mrs. Streng's slightly animated half-face glazed

over to immobility, Zoë defensively clutched the baby tighter when her brother came into the room. Standing ramrod straight, her face became severely taut.

"Excuse me, Mr. Hough-Streng, I must apologize because I'm the one who brought the baby here. I've just come from picking him up and had absolutely no intention of upsetting your mother," I stepped in.

"No, Mrs. Daniel, you do not need to apologize," Zoë said. To her brother, she said gently, "Percival, I asked her to bring Ian in because Mother loves babies. You know that, Perce. She can't get out to participate in anything, and I thought the baby would be perfect to raise her spirits a little."

Percival reigned it in, but only slightly, and said, "No, it makes her tired. Her physical therapist is on his way. Now she won't be able to work to her capacity, and she'll only fall further behind."

"She's too tired. Look at her," he cooed as he walked to her chair, grabbed her hand and petted it. He continued to babble much as a person would to a baby. A bit of emotion passed across Mrs. Streng's face, but it went too quickly to decipher what caused it. Indeed, she did look exhausted, so I took Ian and started out the room. Zoë caught up with me in the hallway.

"I'm sorry for the outburst," she said. "Please bring Ian again. Mother loved seeing him, and so did I."

"Miss Hough-Streng, I don't want to worry your brother. I don't want to delay your mother's recovery any further. He's right; maybe the excitement was too much for her."

"Look, when you come next time, call and make sure I'm here. I'll run interference with Percival, and you can bring the baby. Please? He's so worried about Mother, and he's trying to make sure her recovery is as quick as possible. I, on the other hand, think Ian would be good for her because he could bring her out of herself. She seems so depressed. Please bring him," she pleaded.

"Another thing. My name isn't Hough-Streng. It's just

Streng, Zoë Streng. Percival is my older half-brother. His father was Mother's first husband."

"I wondered about that. I enjoyed the family picture gallery when I first came here and had noticed two different men with your mother, whom I assumed to be two different husbands. Must be nice having an older brother."

"It has been. I missed him so much when he went to boarding school because we had such a nice time together, all four of us. He treated me so well, so caring, just like he is with Mother now. I used to beg him to come home and stay; we all did, but he truly liked boarding school, so we saved all the fun for when he came home."

"Please bring the baby," she said again as we arrived at the door.

While I was strapping Ian in the carseat, a man drove up and parked next to me in the driveway. I didn't recognize him, so I asked, "Are you Mrs. Streng's physical therapist?"

"Yes, how did you know? I just started seeing her last Thursday," he said.

I explained who I was. He told me his name was Seth Garcia. He made sympathy noises for Leticia and said he was vaguely aware of what had happened.

"Mr. Hough-Streng told us you were coming. That's how I guessed who you were." I then asked, "What happened to June Lundberg? I had read in the case file she was working with Mrs. Streng."

He said, "I don't know. We received a call at our clinic requesting a physical therapist to work with Mrs. Streng. They assigned me to the case, and that's all I know. I even had to do the tests over because we received no records of any kind."

With that we parted. I drove to Emily's house, was glee-fully attacked by Jo-Jo and Lulie, my Victorian doll grand-daughters, and had a happy respite from a confusing morning.

Fourteen

HAVING A TODDLER AT THE OFFICE WAS A NOVEL
enough experience that the staff took care of him most of the
remainder of the day, which enabled me to do the paperwork
on Thursday I had intended to do on Wednesday. I also
squeezed in a half-hour to pay some bills. Unfinished business gives me restless nights and monthly bills become that
when they start becoming permanent fixtures on my desk.
Leticia was giving me enough restlessness without the bills
doing that. They all got paid except the one from Department
of Motor Vehicles which needed a smog device certificate
certifying my car as virginally pure of hydrocarbons. Until I
could have the catalytic converter checked, I'd have to pass
on sending in the license renewal. At least DMV was nice
enough to give us a couple months to put off having to get it
okayed.

Ian's and my lunch hour was consumed by errands. I
even managed to fill the gas tank before the warning light came
on. Then it was back to the paperwork quagmire. The boredom
of paperwork is fertile ground for wayward thoughts, and today
my thoughts went the way of Leticia and Seth Garcia's information yesterday. As that tickled my mind, I climbed out of the
paperwork bog two times that day.

The first time, I went to each of the caseworkers and
asked to look at the files of the cases Leticia had been working on. After I read them, I added the names to the master list
of all her cases even though there was nothing irregular
about them. Then I went to the file room to see if any of the
cases were from the drawer that had fallen on Leticia. They
weren't. The cases all came from drawers on the other walls of
the room. I also went to Dolly's logbook to see if anyone had

75

been on the schedule for Leticia to see late the evening she got killed. There wasn't.

The second item on my "Leticia list" was to the call the physical therapy clinic I thought was working with Mrs. Streng. Anne Rivera, the owner of the clinic, had worked other cases with me, and we had a good professional relationship.

"Anne, I'm working with Mrs. Streng and noticed June Lundberg, whom I think is one of your clinicians, is on the case."

"She was. Mrs. Streng's children pulled her off a couple weeks ago. They said their mother wasn't progressing well."

Obviously irritated, she continued, "June is one of our best therapists. I talked to her about the case, and she said the only time there was any follow-through with the assigned exercises was when Leticia Gallegos did the work. The children never seemed to do anything because they claimed it overtired her."

She interrupted herself, "You worked with Leticia, didn't you? I heard about the accident, and I'm sorry. She was a strange bird, if you don't mind my saying. Good with the clients. They liked her, but she could give us holy hell."

"I know what you mean."

"When I tried to talk to the Streng daughter, she became very defensive, claimed she and her brother were their mother's guardians and had decided to quit her therapy for her own good."

"So that fellow over there now is not your clinician?" I asked.

"You mean they have another physical therapist over there?"

When I said yes, she was really annoyed, angry even. "They told me they weren't going to do any more therapy. Even when I told Miss Streng to check with her mother's doctor before making a final decision, she was adamant. We refunded back to the family the money already paid ahead for services and wrote we'd be happy to help Mrs. Streng in the future if they wished."

Thanking her for the information after our well-intentioned, but empty promises to "do lunch", I hung up the phone and added those facts to my developing mental file on Leticia.

When I hurriedly agreed to Mrs. Chu's plan for Ian, it hadn't occurred to me how Woofy might greet him. As I drove home with Ian that first night, my mind ran irrationally rampant with visions of newspaper headlines weeping over the child being mauled by my companionable dog. Except for a few disinterested snorts and a few passing whiffs at Ian, Woofy gave more attention to his bowl of dinner. He was slightly miffed, however, when we got in the car to go get grocery items, and Ian had appropriated his back seat. Woofy solved this dilemma by taking that as permission to come and join me in the front seat, and there he happily sat.

At home that night after Woofy and Ian's walk, I spread a blanket and put Ian on the floor with some toys and books. I then retrieved Mrs. Streng's file which I had conveniently forgotten to return to the office. This time I went through it very carefully. The statements were still clipped to the inside of the chart and appeared to be standard billing invoices with "paid in full" stamped on them. The one for physical therapy services from Anne's clinic was still there. Reading the file intently and slowly yielded little information I hadn't already seen except for the very last page. On the inside cover of the back folder lightly and compactly penciled was my name and phone number.

By the time I made it to the last page, I remembered I had forgotten Ian. No noise from his direction set my thought train screeching with horror again. As I sprang out of the kitchen chair, I knocked it over, practically threw myself across the sofa to where Ian had placed himself, and breathed a sigh of thankful relief. For there on the floor was the sleeping Ian curled in the body crook of a nobly vigilant Woofy.

As I dressed Ian in his nightwear and put him in his borrowed crib, my thoughts returned to Mrs. Streng's chart. The only time Leticia had ever called me at home was that same evening she had also abruptly dismissed me from her house after receiving her phone call. Yet, the next day she wouldn't continue whatever she wished to talk about that Monday which led me to believe that was about the time she had written my name on the chart. Important point? Searching for needles in the ever present haystack? Who knew?

Mrs. Chu called before I left the house the next morning to report her convalescence. Tying to stave off pneumonia, she asked if Ian could stay at my house just a few more days. Having to think about two people, three if I counted Woofy, is energy expending. But, Ian was a sweet kid. He still didn't make noises, but he would smile ever so slightly when I talked to him, and when he saw Woofy, his slight smile would widen almost to a grin. No, it would not be a chore to keep him awhile longer. In fact, it was a gentle time for me because having Ian was a nice reminder of the young lives of my own children.

While standing in front of the open refrigerator, willing it to create a lunch for Ian and me, the phone rang again. This time it was Zoë Streng.

"Mrs. Daniel," she opened hopefully, "your office recep- tionist was kind enough to give me your home number when I explained yesterday who I was. I wanted to catch you before you left. Please, could you bring Ian to see Mother and me? She seemed to enjoy his visit the last time you were here. Please come and bring him. I'll be home all day; I told Percival to go do whatever he wished. That I'd stay with Mother."

"Umm, I believe we can. If you don't hear from me, I'll bring him this morning on my way to the office," I told her.

"Oh, thank you, Mother will be so pleased."

Phone calls slowed my morning routine, so I grabbed the red and white striped shirt waist out of the laundry room, jerked the iron over it like a hurried incantation to erase the wrinkles, hung it in the bathroom in the hope the steam of my bath would get rid of more wrinkles, and danced my slightly wet body into it. Twenty five years ago, I could get ready in ten minutes, bath to finished product. Now it took at least forty-five minutes because I had to use my palette of make-up to artistically contour my age into maturity. Twenty five years ago my auburn hair could fall any which way, and it looked good. Now I had to use my magic wand curling iron to creatively arrange my gray tresses into allure.

Going through the morning machinations of checking Woofy's water bowl, packing Ian's diaper bag, getting his toys and lugging the accoutrements of babyhood to the car, and finally strapping Ian into his carseat, I wondered who would be "so pleased" about seeing Ian again, mama or Zoë.

Fifteen

THE VOICES WEREN'T SCREAMING AT EACH OTHER. They were loud enough to pique my interest into listening, however. It was easy since warm days make for open windows.

Percival was talking, "… I don't care what she says. She's no good anyway. Look at her, nothing is happening; she's withering up like an old lady. We have to do something, or she'll die."

"What do you mean?" asked Zoë. "How can you say that? She has extremely good credentials. She's handled Mother's case well as long as she's been around. I don't want to get rid of her."

"What would you know? You're never around. You leave me here holding the bag, having to care for Mother. Then you blow up when you come here. I have, too, taken good care of her," he said petulantly. "I make sure she gets to her appointments. I feed her. I gave her that room."

"Percival, this is her house," Zoë said patiently. "She should have any room—and any service—she wants. That's not the issue. We have some things to consider before we do anything else."

"Go ahead, say it. I know what you're going to say. You don't think there's enough money. I knew it would get to that; it always does."

"Percival, I said nothing like that. There's plenty of money to take care of Mother; the trustees have assured us of that. I haven't said one word or given any indication that's a problem. You're jumping to unwarranted conclusions. I know you're worried about her. Sometimes I think you're such a good son, you worry too much about her."

There was enough of a pause for them to hear the doorbell. As Zoë answered the front door, I could hear the slamming

81

of a door in another part of the house.

"Mrs. Daniel, how lovely to see you," she said. Years of being ladylike had taught her how to retain her aplomb. There was only a slight tension in her body.

"Did you bring Ian with you?" she asked anxiously.

"Yes, but I left him in the car. I didn't think Mr. Hough-Streng wished him here."

"Oh, dear. You must have heard. I apologize. Percival feels he's borne the brunt of Mother's illness, and, truth to tell, he probably has. At least I have my job at the insurance company, so I can get out of here when it starts getting to me. Poor Perce doesn't have anything like a job to give him a break from all this. He hasn't been able to return to his life because of Mother. The tension and long hours are wearing him down," she said.

As she said this, Percival came from the garage area and, in a controlled manner, said, "Mrs. Daniel, please keep the baby in the car. Mother cannot tolerate any excitement. She's getting weaker by the day."

Zoë answered, "It's all right, Percival. I'll make sure Mother doesn't overdo it today. You go see your friends. Take a break."

"Keep her calm, Zoë. Bye."

"Miss Streng, I feel terrible. I thought when you called that Percival was gone for the day. When I heard you talking, I left Ian in the car, so he wouldn't disturb your brother. I think I should probably leave because I can't stay at your door my whole visit, and I do need to continue to watch him in the car. If your brother doesn't want him to tire your mother, I don't feel I should bring him in."

"Please bring in the baby. It's all right. I know what I'm doing, and there'll be no more arguing. Let's just relax and have a visit with Mother."

I rescued Ian from the confines of the carseat and brought him to Zoë after I nervously checked to assure myself Percival was nowhere in sight. Totally out of character when she saw him, Zoë clapped her hands and virtually squealed with delight. He, on the other hand, grinned and gurgled, the first sounds I had heard him make since I had known him.

Mrs. Streng lifted her head from the pillow when she saw us enter the room, raised her good arm as if to receive the baby and smiled with her half-face.

"Mother, look who came to see you. I asked Mrs. Daniel to bring him here. I could tell you liked Ian when you first met him."

I sat down away from the three of them. Even though Mrs. Streng could not talk, her daughter included her in her conversation while she played with Ian. The child, in turn, grabbed Zoë's hand when she held it up and smiled when she talked to him.

It was a scene from a Mary Cassat painting, the two ladies smiling benignly at Ian. Their attention focused solely on Ian.

While watching the interaction among them, my mind replayed the conversation I had heard this morning. People respond to tension in such different ways. It made me all the more intent on getting as much help as possible for Mrs. Streng, so all three of them could get back to their own lives.

Zoë turned to me, "Mrs. Daniel, Percival won't return until late this evening. Can we please keep him for the day?"

No, that wasn't possible, I thought. The legalities would not allow that, and Charles would have a fit. So, against every rational thought I had, I said, "Yes, why not? I'll pick him up late this afternoon."

And that is how I made it the office, late and less Ian.

Dolly said brightly, "Did the baby go back to Mrs. Chu? I loved having him, but I'm a little behind because I spent so much time with him."

"No," I answered, "Ian is with Miss Streng and her mother. Don't say anything. I know it was unwise to leave him, but they both seem to enjoy him, so I left him there."

"Uh-oh," she began, "Charles is angry today. If you

want to go somewhere, I won't tell him you were here."

"Dolly, you don't have to protect all of us. Charles is just being conscientious. He's put a lot into this agency. I can handle him," I said starting off for his office.

I probably should have taken advantage of Dolly's offer because Charles really blew this time. It started off with my being late and taking charge of a baby who was in the process of becoming a legal pariah.

The declamation then proceeded to, "What in the blazes (Charles thought cursing was *de classe*) gave you the idea to take that baby to the Streng's house? You not only threw their schedule off, you also badly upset their mother. Don't you ever do something as irresponsible as that again. And I mean, never!"

"But, Charles," was all I got out before he bellowed me out his office.

"Get out of here. I will not talk to you now!"

This day was not portending well.

As I walked to my office, Charles' outrage didn't bother me as much as the sympathetically averted heads of my peers.

In my office I spent the first fifteen minutes staring at the desk, pretending I was organizing my schedule. Charles didn't ask about Ian. When he found out where he was, there may not be a roof on the building, and I'd be eating at a soup kitchen. The quandary became whether to call the Strengs, retrieve Ian and have to explain why to them or to risk Charles blowing his stack again.

My decision was no decision, and I didn't get anything done that day either. Didn't even get to a gas station for my smog certificate.

To my abject relief, Percival wasn't home when I returned to pick up Ian. Miss Streng took me back to the sunroom where Ian was actually playing with Mrs. Streng. They were doing the "drop game", the universal children's play that gives new meaning to monotony. The baby drops something; the adult picks it up. Baby drops it again; adult picks it up. And so on. But, Ian's laughing and Mrs. Streng's animation made the game worthwhile to watch. The two were silently communicating.

Being in a bit of hurry to leave, I went to them to get Ian. Mrs. Streng looked receptive enough, so I said, "Mrs. Streng, do you miss Leticia?"

She stopped playing with Ian, looked at me and slightly nodded her head yes.

"Did she give you good care?"

Another slight nod.

"Were you able to talk with her?"

No response. She seemed puzzled.

"Did your son like her?"

Again, no response.

"Did your daughter like her?"

It seemed as though I'd lost her.

"Thanks, Mrs. Streng."

At that, she took the communication board and pointed to the word "don't" and a picture of a door.

Zoë came over, looked at the picture and said, "She's asking you to not leave. She likes Ian."

"I'm sorry, Mrs. Streng. I really do have to leave especially before your son arrives. I'm very sorry."

A slight nod of her head "yes" and a glazed look crusted her eyes.

Sixteen

Mrs. STENG'S FILE WENT WITH ME TO THE OFFICE THE next morning. Between trying to appease Charles by doing paperwork and generally appearing organized, I pored over her file. I had already arranged the invoices chronologically, so I tried to order them alphabetically. None of it seemed to elicit anything, so I decided to call each of the businesses to find out anything they'd tell me.

The first call was to the physical therapist's office. The receptionist at the other end of the phone didn't accept my explanation of why I was entitled to information about Mrs. Streng, so she told me I'd have to send a signed release. That didn't help, so I continued down my list, but the responses from the offices of the occupational therapist, the home health care service, and the ophthalmologist were all the same. Just short of giving up, I tried the phone number on the medical supply invoice.

While I was holding for the owner of the business, I got out the standard release we use for all clients so I could give it to the next Streng I saw to sign for their mother.

"Mrs. Daniel, this is Mr. McAlester. Brent told me you had a question about Mrs. Streng. Does she want this walker?"

"No, not that I know of. Does she not have one?"

"I don't know about that. I only know we had a special order for this walker. There was a deposit on it. I've called the number given, but it's been disconnected. It's sitting here, and I'd like to get it out of the office and be paid the balance."

"I was calling because I found an invoice in a file and wondered why it might be there. Do you know who ordered it?"

"Nah, Brent took the order. Said some gal paid cash for it."

"Do you have any idea who this person was?"

"No, but I need to know what to do with this walker. If you find anything out, let me know, will you?"

"Sure, sure I will," I said as he hung up.

Being office-bound today, I ate lunch with the rest of the staff in the kitchen. The Jail-bail next week was the topic of conversation. They talked about their assignments for the benefit, about their clothes, and they gossiped about who would be there. Charles came in, which he sometimes does when he doesn't have a luncheon engagement, and sat down with the staff to discuss some of the details of the evening. Just as corporate executives and salespeople make some of their most advantageous acquisitions at lunch, so does Charles, the social worker. Probably in an attempt to mollify our last conversation, he asked me if the job I had elected to do was still acceptable to me. If there were something else I'd rather do, he'd do his best to arrange it.

"No," I said. "Taking tickets and money will be fine. I can get in and out quickly."

"I understand, Mrs. Daniel. But I hope you don't feel attending this function unaccompanied will be awkward. There are many of us who are single."

"Oh, I don't think that's a problem," I lied. "I expect my daughter and son-in-law will be there, so I won't be alone."

"Oh, marvelous! They are always so supportive of our community projects. It will be nice to renew our acquaintance again," he said solicitously as he gracefully edged out of the room.

Dolly sat beside me and said to Genevieve and Jill, "You know what I'll miss at this function?"

Gen asked "What?"

"I'll miss Leticia."

Shocked, Jill said, "Why?"

"Oh, she always dressed so well. She saw to all the details. Her shoes and purse matched. Her hair was done so well. You know, Louisa, how she swept it up. And, wow ... she always had the most glamorous dresses."

"Sure, if you like the whore look," spat out Gen.

"Genny," I said, "didn't your mama teach you about speaking ill of the dead."

As Gen shot me a supercilious glance, Dolly continued, "No, really. She had guts. She could wear anything and look good. You're probably right about the whore look, but you have to admit she looked as spectacular as some of those old Hollywood mega-stars."

As Gen's face turned sour, Dolly turned to me and changed the subject before Gen could make another comment about Leticia. "Louisa, remember when you walked by the file room the other day and asked me about the stool?"

"Yes."

"What was that all about?"

"I'm not sure. Something just struck me at the time. It didn't make sense that that stool would be intact. If Louisa were really filing, then it should have been crushed or, at least, bent."

Jill, who had been intently listening said, "You can't be saying ...Louisa, are you saying she was killed? That's impossible. No one, I mean, people didn't like her. But no one would murd—Oh, that's crazy."

"But, Jill, " Dolly said. "That *was* weird. Maybe Louisa is right." Turning to me, she asked, "Did you tell anyone about the stool?"

"I talked with Lt. Washburn. Basically, he said what you just did, Jill. He was indulgent. Did you know he's been promoted? And, you know what?"

"What?" all three said in unison.

However, before I could finish my thought, Genevieve got that sharp look in her eye and interrupted by saying, "Why, Louisa Daniel, I believe you've got stars in your eyes. What could that possibly mean for Lt. Washburn?"

That was enough to stop the conversation.

That afternoon, Leticia's old boyfriend, Kelly, was in the parking lot again. I couldn't tell if he was Jill's new boyfriend. Gen hadn't approved the status, and Jill never discussed it, so he was hard to pigeonhole. He looked up when he became aware of me, and we were close enough that I could see the squint in his eyes. Being alone in the parking lot with him made me skittish, and I hurried to my car without saying anything.

I had asked Gen if he were a mechanic, but she said she heard he managed a health club at night, and that enabled him to keep his self-appointed dates with the parking lot after work hours. His nicely toned body was also nicely tanned. It was a true tone, too, not a miscellaneous combination of steroid pillows.

He slid down into the car seat when he saw me. He was in Jill's car.

Seventeen

ZOË HAD BROUGHT MRS. STRENG TO THE BACK PORCH when I went to their house that evening. Sunshine had not just bathed us today; it had baked us. The usual summer weather cycle was three days of warmth and three days of cool, and it looked like we were slipping into that pattern. Those hot afternoons made for pleasant evening nights as the ocean breezes hurdled the Oakland hills and slowly overpowered the torrid, incandescent temperature of the afternoon from the valleys to the east.

Even though Zoë had seen to her dressing and hair, Mrs. Streng had the look of a day after Christmas bow. She sat listlessly in the chair and stared at nothing. Even her floral silk loungers appeared wilted. She didn't even look at me when I asked her how she was doing.

"Miss Streng," I asked "do you know anything about a walker ordered for your mother?"

She paused. "No, I haven't heard anything. Percival hasn't said anything. Why?"

"There were some invoices in Mrs. Streng's file that Leticia had kept. I called the phone number on each of them in an attempt to find out what they were doing there. Nobody would give me any information because they wanted signed releases. However, the man at the medical supply said there was a special order walker for your mother."

"No, I don't know. I'll ask Percival, though. If you want any releases, I'll sign them. Leave one here, and I'll get it to you soon."

"Thanks, I'd like to hear what they have to say."

Out of the corner of my eye, I noticed a movement in the wheel chair. Mrs. Streng seemed to straighten momentarily, but then she lapsed back to her flaccid state.

"Mrs. Streng, do you know anything about the walker?"

A slight movement of her eyes was the only answer she gave.

I knelt down to look directly into her face and said, "Mrs. Streng, I wish you would talk. Whenever I come, you make me feel like I'm in a puzzle."

She looked at me then and lifted the one corner of her mouth. A smile or starting to say a word? I couldn't tell.

Percival strolled onto the patio, looked at me and said, "You didn't bring that child, did you?"

"No, he's with my daughter. He really is a nice little boy, you know."

"That may be, but he upsets Mother, and we can't have that. She must get well."

"I understand your concern. It seemed to me that your mother enjoyed his company. Maybe having Ian around would make your mother see the value of getting well."

"No," he said emphatically. "He must never come here again. I told that to Mr. Overton, and he agreed with me."

Of course, Charles would agree with you, you twerp. He doesn't want to lose one of his most prestigious clients. I only said, "I thought it might have been you who made a complaint. Charles has made sure I will not bring Ian again."

"Percival, what did you do?" interjected Zoë.

"What do you mean what did I do? I did what you should have done. You can't allow anything in this house to upset Mother. She's so frail right now. Maybe later, she can see the little boy, but not now. I went to that agency and told them if that kid showed up at this house one more time, I'd pull their contract. It is ridiculous to even think that this old woman should have a crying toddler around her. It just upsets me!"

"Percival, that's enough," Zoë said quietly but with enough sureness that he stopped immediately and left the porch.

Mrs. Streng closed her eyes and slumped forward in her

chair. We both went to her and Zoë took her hand and said "I'm sorry, Mother."

She opened her eyes. Tears had already started to well up. Zoë held her. Only a slight shudder told us she was crying. I accompanied them as Zoë wheeled her mother to her bed. On the way there, Zoë started to explain Percival's concern for his mother.

"Percival was so much older than me. His father was Mother's first husband, but he left them when Percival was four. She had her family's money and this house, so she was able to care for him. She married my dad about five years later. He enjoyed having Percival as a son, so he made sure Percival was raised the same as he.

"He was at boarding school when I was born. Needless to say, I was a surprise. Mother was almost forty; Daddy was fifty. It was nice though because Percival was a wonderful older brother. I use to beg them to let him come home all the time, but he wanted to stay at school because he said he had his friends there. It was also a good prep school for the university he wanted to attend. Boy, I used to miss him. I guess I already told you that, didn't I?"

She went on, "When Daddy died, Percival changed. He was so upset about losing him. It seems little things upset him so much more now. He really needed Daddy.

"I'm sorry he told your boss about the baby. If there's anything I can do to alleviate the situation, I will," she added.

"No, I'm fine. I shouldn't have brought the baby in the first place. Charles is right on that account. He's a good person, but he's under pressure to make sure the agency runs well, and every once in awhile, he blows. Just like the rest of us. It will be fine, but thank you for the concern."

We put Mrs. Streng in her bed. I held her hand and said good-bye, to which she gave a slight squeeze.

On the way out, Zoë asked me to contact Dr. Cannaughton and see if she could relay any information to me about her mother's condition to pass on to her brother and her.

She felt Dr. Cannaughton might respond to another professional and give more information than she would to a family member.

"She only seems to get worse," Zoë said. "There's nothing
to raise her spirits. That's one of the reasons I wanted you to
bring Ian. She seemed to like him so much. See if there's anything else we can do, please."

After I seated myself in the car, I realized Zoë still hadn't
signed the release.

Eighteen

"STAY FOR DINNER, MOM. THE GIRLS WILL BE HOME soon from swim practice, and they'd like to see you," Emily said when I went to pick up Ian.

"That would be nice, thanks."

"When's Mrs. Chu going to get back?"

"Is Ian too much? You know you don't have to take him," I said.

I looked at her standing at the counter, chopping greens for a salad. Not a beauty, but beautiful. She was one of those women who melded into a crowd; there was nothing physically outstanding about her. Her personality crept out her pores so that one day a person would look at her and wonder how she was missed in the once-over of the crowd. Not model thin, but well formed, she wore clothes as though they were made only for her, not bought off the rack at the local department store. Her family could have easily been the next door neighbors of the Cleavers; there wasn't a germ of dysfunction among it.

"No, I'm thinking about you. You look exhausted. He's no problem. JoJo and Lulie really like him. They like him so much they're after us to have a baby brother."

I laughed, "What did you tell them?'

"I said all four of us are too old to have a baby, and their baby is the dog."

"I take it the fur and bark come from David's side of the family?"

"That's what he said, too. So when do you get to relax?"

"I don't think the baby is what's making me tired. You remember Leticia Gallegos, the one who was killed? I think that's what's getting to me," I said.

"I remember the accident. Are you still wondering about the stool?" Emily asked.

"I am. I talked to Lt. Washburn about it. He was the investigator the day of the accident. Do you remember his kids? You and your brother went to school with them."

"Yeah, they were nice people. Bob Jr. was great looking and a terrific basketball player. Made all-state."

"That's right. I'd forgotten. So back to Leticia. Dolly asked me about the stool at lunch yesterday, and the office thinks I'm bordering on paranoia to even mention that she might have been killed.

"There's the boyfriend. I knew about him, but I didn't. You know what I mean? I'd see him but not really put him with anyone. He was kind of a fixture because he kept hanging around the office—still does. Actually he's hanging around Jill now, and she's doing nothing to stop him. Genevieve can't stand him because she just knows he's going to beat Jill to a pulp.

"And, then there's Mrs. Streng. She's an agency board member, but she's had a stroke. Leticia was working with her, now I've got the case. She's got a son who worries all the time. He carries on about how his mother needs all this care. He is so concerned about her. Both the son and daughter are, really. Zoë is more relaxed than Percival; he's a very nervous type. Very unhappy with me because I brought Ian over to the house. He told Charles who laid into me. That was embarrassing. Charles likes to get after me anyway. He's always harping about my being late or behind on paperwork."

"But you're a good worker. He knows how valuable you are to the agency. I thought he likes you. Everytime David or I see him he talks about how wonderful you are for the agency."

"Oh, he does. He'd like me better if I had a graduate degree or two. But, you know, he does it to others of us. We each have a "Charles phase" where he singles us out and verbally skewers us because we don't have advanced degrees. It's good we three are some of his best caseworkers; he'd really have a field day if we weren't. When a person lives and breathes a goal, he tends to want to make it the best it can be. And that's Charles. To be the best social work agency in town, there is no room for error."

Byte, their German Shepherd, heralded the arrival of the family by barking and running in, running out and running back in, barking all the while.

"Okay, okay." Em patted her on the head. Her announcement completed, Byte sat on the floor, letting her back legs slide out from under her to groan into a curled position.

The granddaughters ran in; smacked juicy kisses on my cheeks, and sat wet bathing suit marks on my gray silk jump suit. Both had matching team swimsuits on and chlorine green blond hair, but that was the only way in which they were similar. Seven year-old JoJo wore her suit with the proud decorum of a young army officer while Lulie's bathing suit hung on her bean pole body like overstretched elastic.

"How was your day, sweet potatoes?" I asked.

"Well," declared JoJo in her very precise speech, "I had to carefully explain to Lulie that she doesn't do 'threestyle' and 'catch-up' strokes. It is 'freestyle', and 'catch-up' isn't even a stroke. It's just a way to practice swimming. Having to explain made us late to get out, and Daddy had to wait a long time."

"Daddy didn't mind, JoJo," Lulie reminded her. Her bathing suit dripped down her body, so the back looked like she had an extra bottom. "He said it was okay. Anyway, you're wrong, it is a 'threestyle'. The coach said it was." She squeezed her little face into defiance at JoJo's setting her straight.

"You are wrong, and I am right," JoJo matched her in insolence. Just as Lulie opened her mouth to escalate the confrontation, David came in. David's kiss was not as juicy as his daughters' were, but just as welcoming.

"I got that contract! We're going out to dinner." Looking at me, he smiled. "All of us."

The little girls squealed off to their room to change.

Nineteen

Dr. CANNAUGHTON TOOK THE PHONE FROM THE receptionist and said, "I told her to put you through if you called again. I wanted to tell you I'm no longer handling Mrs. Streng's case."

I was shocked, "Why not?"

"I received a letter from the children asking that records be sent to the hospital. That's where she will be receiving all her care from now on."

"Who signed it?"

"The names of both children were on the signature block."

"I'm at a loss. A few days ago I heard a disagreement between Mrs. Streng's children. They were arguing about someone being off the case because they could see no progress. Do you want me to say anything to them?"

"No, I don't think that would be ethical."

"Before you hang up, can you tell me why Mrs. Streng seems to get worse? That's the reason I called."

"I don't think she's getting worse. I think she's not improving, so she's becoming depressed. Frankly, Mrs. Daniel, I think something is blocking any attempt for her to get better. At first I thought the excuses about her being too tired to go to appointments were acceptable. Now, I'm not so sure."

"One more question. Who has paid for your services?"

"The children asked that we bill in advance, so they could send it to the insurance company. Said it would be easier for the trustees to bill that way. We'll notify the company that billing for services should be reduced. These people don't have the standard health plan insurance. They have some private insurance that goes through the family trust, I believe."

Puzzled, I sat until the call from Mrs. Chu came in saying

she was ready for Ian to come home. I listened half-heartedly as she bombarded me in her chirping voice with how much she had missed her kids and, most especially, Ian.

"Right, Mrs. Chu, I'll bring him to you tonight."

With ambivalent feelings, I drove to Emily's house to pick up Ian. I was going to miss him; his quiet little presence was reassuring to have around. Woofy would probably be happy to have his back car seat to himself, but then again, maybe not. He was beginning to enjoy the view from the passenger's seat. He would miss having the baby to roll him a ball, though.

"Emily," I said as I put the baby gear in the car, "are you going to the Jail-Bail Saturday."

"Oh, yes, David has tickets through Rotary. You gave me the tickets you bought, and I can also get them through Junior League. It seems every local charity is gearing up for this, so it should raise a hefty amount of money. Are you going?"

"I'm working at the check-in desk as a banker."

"Do you want to go with us, or will you pull your usual first-in, first-out?"

"Yes, probably. No, don't pick me up. I'll see you there."

"If you stick around long enough," she said as she closed my car door.

At Mrs. Chu's, Ian waved at me when I told him good-bye. He even smiled a little and seemed to mouth "bye" to me. Holding him out to Mrs. Chu, he went to her willingly. He was making progress.

Zoë took the release I handed to her at the conclusion of a visit to her mother. "I'll get this to you soon."

I said, "I talked with Dr. Cannaughton yesterday."

"Any information?"

"She said she was no longer on the case. That you and your brother had terminated her services."

"That's not so." She didn't seem surprised about it.

"You didn't know about it?"

"No, I'll have to look into it." She seemed nervous, and didn't appear inclined to pursue the discussion.

I told her what else the physician had said. She didn't make much comment and said she would be more aware of appointment times. I walked myself to the door because Zoë seemed disinclined to escort me.

Twenty

THE HILLS WERE LOOKING DERMATOLOGICALLY DISEASED with their splotches of green and brown. If the days stayed as warm as today was getting, it would only be a few days until they would be wearing their summer tan.

The warmth of the day begged for the cool of the air conditioner. As the car cooled, I thought about the conversation with Emily. That led to ruminations about work, which led to thoughts about Leticia. The invoices must be the key. No one had complained of non-payment. Yet some of the services were discontinued. Why would someone order an appliance and not pick it up?

As I tried to piece all this together, I decided I'd better get gas and started to look for a station. Unfortunately there was no gas station conveniently perched on the top of the hills through which I was driving. It might be a toss-up to see whether I would be pumping gas in twenty minutes or waiting by the side of the road for help. Many times I had watched the red arrow point accusingly to the "E" on my gas gage. Many times I had watched the "low fuel light" leering at me. But never yet had I been stuck by the side of the road waiting for some highway angel to bring me gasoline. I turned the air conditioner lower because it was stuffy. I was getting sleepy. All I wanted was to get to the gas station. In a few minutes, I'd crest the hill and the few remaining fumes of gasoline would be able to float me into the station.

At times like these I curse my ex-husband. He used to keep the car filled. In the division of marital labor, it was his job to take care of transportation. If he hadn't left, I wouldn't be in this predicament. I was tired and got so mad at him. If I didn't make it to that station and had to walk to get gas, it would be his fault. It would be his fault that I would be late getting to the office. It would be his fault Charles would get after me again. It all would be his fault.

The oncoming car made me veer back into my own lane, snapping me out of my frustration with my ex-husband. I couldn't keep my eyes open. I felt like my head was full of a cloud, vapor floating in no particular direction. There was a station coming up; just a few minutes and I'd be there if I could keep my eyes open and not fall asleep.

Arriving at the gas station, I sat in the car awhile while trying to accumulate enough energy to open the car door and get out to pump gas. Finally, the attendant came over and tapped on the window. I opened the door.

"Ma'am," he said, "this is self-serve. If you want me to pump, you have to go to the other side of the pumps."

Mumbling "sorry", I got out. Walking around seemed to eradicate the sleepiness, and I bought a Dr. Pepper hoping the caffeine would jump-start my brain into alertness. It worked for a bit, but driving to the office in the warm car, I was aware of the listlessness coming back.

Jill must have noticed it also because she asked when I came in, if I were all right.

"I think so," I said. "There's so much on my mind; guess I'm thinking too hard."

She looked puzzled. "Leticia's death is just so confusing. It's been hard on a lot of us, you know?"

"Do you want to talk about it?"

She hesitated and then said, "No, it will be fine. Thank you though." She left.

Charles came in and waited while I finished a phone conversation with a client.

He started in, "Mrs. Daniel, I want to talk with you concerning…"

I thought I could maintain my professionalism; I really thought I could do it. Maybe the fatigue precipitated my tirade.

"Charles, if you've come to tell me I'm late again or that my paperwork isn't in, please don't. I'm in no mood for being singled out. You are so driven by this agency and making it the best, you forget you have people who are, in their own ways, trying just as hard as you to do a job well. There is not one person here who isn't a fine worker. It doesn't matter what kind of degree they have. When I went to school, it was a feat for a woman to get even one degree. You've placed so much emphasis on an advanced degree being the criterion of excellence, you've forgotten the value of years of experience. That experience isn't just sitting at a desk; it's doing all the grunt work, too."

It was getting visceral. My gut was in a visegrip of muscle. "Look, Charles. At forty I lost my husband. At fifty, I lost my figure. I'll be damned if I'm going to lose my job at sixty. You can harass me all you want, I'll get an attorney here and file an age discrimination suit before you can call an emergency board meeting."

As I loaded up my lungs to continue, he held out his hands in a defensive stance and said placatingly, "Mrs. Daniol, Louisa, please calm down. I'm sorry you feel I've been persecuting you. You are correct in saying we have an excellent staff here. It appears you've been misreading my intentions. I do not condemn you for your lack of further education. I only wish to point out ways you may achieve further quality in your already excellent work. I would hate to see anyone with the skills you possess become ineffective by not having further schooling in the newest and latest counseling techniques. You must accept my apologies if I appeared to be anything but concerned for you. I will attempt to relay to the rest of the staff my concern for them and their duties."

He smeared his unctuousness as thickly as peanut butter on a sandwich. I tried not to look dumbfounded, but that was difficult. It was also difficult to ignore the small throng at the door of my office. When Charles seemed to finish talking, they started backing away.

"Go home," he said sympathetically. "You look tired. Try

and relax for the rest of the afternoon. By the way, I only came in to talk to you concerning your job as banker for the Jail-Bail," he smiled.

"Right, okay. Thanks, Charles."

Twenty One

MINUTES LATER I WENT OUT TO THE PARKING LOT STILL in dazed annoyance at Charles' and my encounter. Just before getting into my car I noticed Kelly slinking out of the back of the parking lot. Still pumped up from having stood up to Charles, I thought I'd give Paul Bunyan a warning. I didn't give a shit what he did. I figured I was mad enough and tall enough to let him have it with a briefcase to the side of the head if he made one move toward me.

"Kelly, wait." That only made him slink faster.

"Wait! I want to tell you something."

He paused, turned. As I approached him, I could see him slightly, looking me warily in the eye.

A sullen "What do you want?"

"Look, Kelly. You should be warned. Charles is bent way out of shape. He's on every one of us like a rodeo rider on a bucking bull. He said he'd get on to you if you kept hanging around here."

Not adding that people thought he had something to do with Leticia's death, I took a deep breath, waiting to flood him with my frustration.

"Mrs. Daniel, police have questioned me; people in the office give me funny looks. I have no idea what happened to Leticia. I never hurt her."

"How can you say that? I saw the bruises."

"Leticia was a friend. She was the one who got me tied in with a drug rehab program and helped me everytime I couldn't stay with it. I could go to her apartment anytime I needed. No one, except Jill, understands that." He paused and then said, "Even she has trouble with it."

"Come on, Kelly. You don't think that's a wee bit out of

line?" Contempt dripped like sludge down a landslide. "We saw the bruises. You lurk around here like me and my shadow. We know you like the sauce, so what's the deal?"

"I haven't had alcohol for two years—as long as I've worked with Leticia. I haven't hit her. I'd never hurt her."

I've done social work for thirty-five years. Like a good cop, priest or psychiatrist, a good social worker develops a gut feeling for truth and lies. My gut told me this guy was telling the truth.

"Okay, Kelly."

He started to walk away from me when something he said hit me. Like a broken record I said, "Hey, wait."

This time when he turned to me, the wariness was gone. "You said something," I started. "You said you could go to Leticia's apartment anytime. Was she always there when you went?"

"No, I'd just let myself in. It was a nice place to go. Sometimes I'd sit and stare. Sometimes I'd watch movies. She never had any liquor in the place, so I knew if I could get there and stay, I could talk myself out of a drink."

"Does that mean you have a key to her place? Have you been over there since?"

"Sure, rent is paid for two more months. Leticia paid six months in advance. The police are out. I don't think they found anything. I still go over once in awhile," he responded.

I asked, "Would you do me a big favor and let me go into the apartment? You can take me there and go in with me, but would you let me look around? Please?" I hated begging especially when not twenty minutes earlier I was ready to crucify this guy for just hanging around.

"Sure. I don't have a class until this evening, so I'll wait for you in the car or go in with you—whatever you want."

I said, "How about different cars? I can go do a couple field calls afterward, and I won't hold you up."

"Yeah, sure."

Maybe he knew more than he was admitting. Maybe this

wasn't too smart going off with him. If I stepped in the office and told someone where I was going, I might feel safer. However, he got in his car and started driving out, so I hustled over to my car and proceeded to follow Kelly to Leticia's house. In the half-hour drive, I decided it was prudent to leave Kelly in his car when we got there. It might be safer that way. I didn't want to get caught in the upheaval of whatever might set him off.

As it was, that was his proposal also. So he stayed in the car and waited while I went into Leticia's apartment.

I opened the door to Leticia's designers' showcase. As in my other visit, nothing was out of place, no pictures, no magazines or newspapers, and no dirty dishes. Walking to the kitchen, I started to open the cabinet to see if her cabinets were as tidy as the rest of her home when I heard a step. At least, I thought I heard it. My guilt from sneaking around must be getting the better part of my underhandedness.

In the cabinet I found a box of cereal and the carrion of a banana bedeviled by fruit flies. That, a few glasses and some plastic microwave plates were the only items. It might be interesting to find out how long Leticia had used this address because she didn't seem to have moved in completely.

As I turned to cross the dining area to the bedroom, I called out Kelly's name because I know I heard him this time. It became unnerving and frightening that he should not answer. I retraced my path through the house to make sure Kelly was still in the car. When I didn't find him, I looked out the living room and saw a head in Kelly's car, so I figured I must have been hearing things. The front door was still locked as were the sliding glass doors, so I knew I must be hearing things.

In the bedroom, I had just opened one of the desk drawers when my skull banged against my cortex, and my eyes saw a gray square punctuated by moving stars. As I slid down the dresser I marveled at the fact that a smash on the head could so thoroughly annihilate consciousness.

Twenty Two

COME ON, EYES, OPEN! OPEN, NOW! BUT THEY WOULDN'T, and they needed to because I kept hearing my name. My eyes needed to open, so they could see the direction of the name. My ears couldn't see it. Open, eyes, open! My neck was gone. There was only a spring holding up my head, and it wouldn't stay in one direction. If my eyes would open, I could get my neck back, and my head wouldn't hurt. Then the name would get closer, and I could see its caller.

As my head bobbled on its flimsy neck, my eyes tried so hard to open. The name was louder, but then it got softer. Maybe if I leave it alone, it'll come back.

Finally when my eyes did open, I saw Kelly, and he gave me some water. If I could have lifted off my head and replaced it with a new one, I would have done so because the pain was so violent it reached down to my stomach and started churning it.

I started to ask him why, but I couldn't remember what the why was about. He kept asking if I was all right. "Of course, I am," I said. "Why? Why … I can't remember. Why?"

"Mrs. Daniel," Kelly said. He sounded like that voice I had heard earlier. "I waited an hour in the car. You didn't came out, so I came to see what had happened. The door was open, and you were lying on the bedroom floor. Are you hearing what I'm saying?"

"Yes, I hear. But why didn't you answer me? I heard you— a couple times. I called your name. Why didn't you answer?"

"Mrs. Daniel, I wasn't here. I waited in the car. Don't you remember? I said I'd wait. You said I could leave if I wanted. You'd get the key back to me. Don't you remember?" he asked.

"Wait, just a minute. Let me think. Give me some time."

My mind had to go inside itself and pick something out of a corner. It was like finding a lost, dark, sock stuffed at the back of the closet. We waited. He sat while I tried to retrieve my memory.

He had helped me onto Leticia's bed and propped up my head and neck with pillows. If I hadn't been so woozy, I might have dwelt on the thought of dead Leticia being the last one in this bed. Maybe the sheets hadn't even been changed, and there would still be some smell of her life in them. But, my thoughts were tumbling over a cliff, and I banished Leticia from my mind and watched Kelly waiting patiently while my neck reattached itself to my body. It probably wasn't more than a few minutes while I lay there, but it felt as though the afternoon had slid past us. Eventually, I remembered why I was there, and what I had seen.

"Kelly, when you come here, what do you do? There's nothing to eat. This place looks like Leticia never moved in," I said as I slowly brought my knees over the side of the bed and took in the details of the bedroom.

The bedroom brandished as much quiet ostentation as the living and dining rooms, but instead of using color as in those rooms, Leticia had used texture. On the brass poster bed was a white satin coverlet and duster; and on the crossbeams of the four poster bed was a white filmy canopy draped at an angle. The only chair in the room wore a white linen slipcover with pillows of the same satin as the bed coverlet. The windows were covered in the same linen edged in white satin. Leticia's only nod to contrast was the black lacquer dresser. All this stood on a looped, wool, white carpet. This room was more in keeping with Leticia's personality than the living area. Crisp and stark just like the woman herself.

To satisfy my curiosity I cautiously, so as not to jar my aching head anymore, stepped into the bathroom. As Kelly reached out to steady me on my rubber legs, he said, "Maybe you should go to the hospital. We can come back anytime. Your age—" he stammered a revision after I gave him a warning glance. "I mean, maybe you, well, you know, you had quite a blow to your head and should get it checked. I'll take you to the hospital."

"No, that's all right. I want to look in here."

For its size, the bathroom could have been the second parlor, and it, too, was white and brass although there were towels of the same taupe, black and gray used in the living areas. The bathroom was glamorous, but it, too, was impersonal like Leticia.

Back in the bedroom, we found some linens, accessories for the clothes hanging in the closet, and shoes. A few of the spring and summer clothes still had store tags on them, but there were no winter clothes other than a few sweaters. Even though I had seen her wear winter clothes, Leticia only had late spring and summer clothes in her closet. She had obviously recently shopped for her new season wardrobe, but she must have had some winter clothes somewhere. No one I know of gets rid of her clothes after one season, but in all the searching we did, we found nothing old. The dresser drawers where she kept her lingerie yielded frothy opulence. Her desk had some pencils and blank paper. There were no bills. There were no receipts. No checkbooks.

"I'm not trying to be nosy, Kelly, but did you ever look in her drawers or closet before? I'm only asking because this is odd. There's hardly anything in these cabinets? Do these look like you remember them?"

"The only time I looked in a cabinet was when I needed some tissues. There weren't any in the kitchen or bath. There were some supplies, bars of soap, detergent, tissues, so I didn't look anywhere else."

I was discovering more empty facts, confusing as they were, about Leticia now that she was dead than I had known when she was alive. I wandered back with Kelly to the kitchen. We went through the cabinets one more time, but they were just as bare as before. As I reached out my hand to remove the decrepit banana, I knocked the cereal box over. It was partially empty, so I decided to take it and the banana to the trash at my house. Leaving the food here would only draw more flies.

We closed the door and locked it. Approaching our cars, I beeped open the car doors and threw the trash in the back.

"You know, Kelly, I called for you a couple times back there. Did you not hear me?"

"Mrs. Daniel, how could I? Like I told you, I was in the car the whole time until I found you lying against that dresser. What made you think I was in there?"

"I heard noises, footsteps, I thought."

"You all right, Mrs. Daniel? You look awfully pale. Maybe I should take you to the hospital. You should have that head checked."

"No, I don't need to go to the hospital. My head hurts, but if it gets worse, I'll go see my doctor."

It was unnerving that Kelly didn't see anyone. At least, that's what he said.

Quickly, before I realized what he was doing and could stop him, he got in the passenger side of my car. When he did that my senses flashed warnings, and I held my breath backing up against the door, so my hand would be close to the door handle. I held my breath and tried to recall self-defense methods for women.

He didn't say anything. His massive body filling the right side of the car so much so it seemed his knees were going to jab his chin, he sat there looking at me intently, making no other move. I tried to visualize what I should do next. If I grabbed the door handle, would it open fast enough for me to tumble out? Where would I run? If he came at me, then what? Visualizing a plan of attack only made my head pulsate more.

He didn't appear to notice my jumpy jitters because all he wanted was to talk. "I manage an all night sports and fitness club," he started. "You'd be surprised how many people use the place at odd hours. Some clients wait until then because there aren't many people around, so it's easier to get to use the equipment. Some of them come in after their night shift. There are a few women, nurses from the hospitals, programmers, those kinds of ladies, but most of the people are men. I remember the first time I ever saw Leticia. You know how beautiful she was. She came in for the 5:00 A.M. morning aerobics class wearing four-inch heels, a black Spandex leotard and tights, and a silver sequined belt and headband. At that hour in the morning, seeing her, most of the people just stopped. There were all kinds of clangs because they let the weights, and their teeth, just drop. She even started doing aerobics in those heels. At least, she did the warm up that way.

"Then she stopped about ten minutes into the hour, took off her shoes and put on her workout shoes and socks. The way she did it, she gave all the guys a hard-on," he chuckled to himself when he said this.

"Excuse me, Mrs. Daniel," Kelly said checking himself. "I'm just trying to tell you how I met her. She would always do it that way, about three times a week. She never smiled. She came in, got her locker key, warmed up in her very high heels and turned all the guys on with a striptease of her shoes and socks.

"Finally after a few weeks, I started talking to her. She didn't really carry on much of a conversation. She just looked at me while I kind of teased her and left when I ran out of jokes.

"Then one night she came in after I had been drinking really bad. She'd been coming almost a year. I was shitfaced, totally out of it. The boss was there that time because I was late, so the manager on the shift before mine called him. The boss was laying into me and told me if I didn't straighten up I would not only lose the job, he'd make sure I never got another one dealing with sports in the Bay Area. My whole life is athletics, and I couldn't live and not be around sports.

"Leticia waited around and followed me out of the complex. It was strange the way she came up to me. She never asked me how I was, or what I wanted to do. She just said, 'I'll help you.' That was it, nothing else."

"That's Leticia," I said. "She never much cared what other people wanted. She figured she had the answers."

"That may be true. In my case, she did. She made me straighten up, and, because of that, I kept my job. She was a good friend. There were times she was moody, but that was okay with me."

"Thanks," I said finally.

"What for?"

"It helps. What you told me helps. There were times I was furious with Leticia. Every time my anger got the best of me, there would be an incident where she had assisted someone, and it made me again realize she had a unique talent for being helpful. Sometimes I thought she was so cold she could freeze water, but for people who needed her, her warmth was unending. She was an enigma.

"Hey, Kelly," I asked as he opened the door to unbend out of my car," do you have a last name? As long as I've seen you around, I don't even know your name."

"Yeah," he grinned, "It's Powell, and thanks for asking."

With that he walked to his car, got in, and drove off.

Visiting Leticia's apartment had consumed the rest of the day. This was bad because there could be no field visits; it was good because traffic wouldn't be heavy, and I'd get home at a reasonable time. Oddly enough, I didn't really feel it had been a wasted day because Kelly had provided some insight into Leticia's personality. He had also turned out to be a pleasant fellow, and, for that I promised myself I'd have lunch with the staff just to put in two cents of good gossip about him.

This drive was long enough for deep thinking. I also realized how tired I was. That bump on the head must be harder to revive from than I thought. If my gut feeling about Kelly were wrong, and he wasn't telling the truth, then I couldn't trust the gut anymore. If he were the one who knocked me out, then he's lying. I know there was someone in the apartment, but since people work during the day, there probably would not be anyone around to see Kelly if he had gone in and out of the condo.

And what about Leticia? I knew Kelly hadn't hit her. Did I really, or is my gut deceiving me? I only know that because he told me, but, then, Leticia never really said he hit her. She let us conclude it, that's all. Okay, so what do I know? She must not like to eat; that's one way to stay slim. She only had spring and summer clothes, some still new. Kelly said she paid her rent six months in advance. She had no bills or receipts or checkbook. I wonder if the police found paperwork and took it? Yet, even if they had, I would never know because I had no in's at the police department. She may have paid for everything in cash which is a lot of cash to have at one time.

Thoughts like this carouseled through my mind until I drove into my driveway. Woofy must have been bored waiting so long for me because he didn't run to greet me. Instead he walked in and looked at me with morose eyes.

"Don't you start in on me. I've had a day and a half. After your walk, we go directly to bed."

The walk mollified him, but it only churned the day's events in my head harder. Sleep that night was deep and a welcome respite from thinking.

Twenty Three

I GLANCED AT THE CLOCK AS I LOPED OUT THE DOOR laden with my briefcase, purse and lunch. Was the office going to be amazed! I was going to arrive an hour early today. Falling asleep so early after that club on the head forced me awake at four in the morning. It was too hard to return to the oblivious comfort of sleep, so I puttered around the house, got myself ready, took Woofy for a long constitutional and decided to beat it to the office.

Opening the back car door to dump my morning burden, there was a pungent banana smell, and I remembered the wizened banana and the cereal box I had intended to throw in the garbage last night. I gingerly picked up the leaking banana by its stem to pack it in the cereal box. Just as I started to pull apart the box to stuff the fruit in, I noticed an envelope situated between the wax paper and the cardboard. Although there had been no mention of a prize on the cereal box, I thought I'd take it because Lulie liked miniature toys and junk.

Upon inspection it was an envelope with several pieces of paper in it. Most of the sheets had lines with several letters and numbers, the same number of letters and numbers on each line. There were also three or four invoices that were copies of the ones in Mrs. Streng's chart in the envelope. The speech therapy clinic, the medical supply business, and physical therapy clinic were all represented. There was also a contract from an audiologist's office. After putting the papers back into the envelope, I filed it in my purse to examine closely at the office and went back to the house to toss the garbage.

I stopped at the boarding home to see Ian and Mrs.Chu. The extra weight Ian had gained added health to his cheeks

119

and shine to his blond curls. Although his expression was still unsure, he, at least, seemed to be smiling. Mrs. Chu reported some attempts at words, and that Ian was letting her know when he was unhappy.

At the office, I asked Charles if he had heard anything from the court regarding Ian. Initially we had questions about his chances of being adopted, but now I wasn't so sure. Maybe with the right foster home, he was young enough that his pitiable initiation into life could be overcome. Charles said the natural parents were considering giving up their rights to him. They felt the legal system might not deal as harshly with them if they could not influence Ian in anyway. We would continue to board him as a foster child for the state until some decision could be made, and I was to continue following the case. I liked hearing that. I liked it because it was hopeful for Ian, and it meant I could continue to be with him and watch him progress.

In my own office, I got the envelope from my purse and spread the papers on my desk. On the back of each of the invoices, I put everything I could remember about each business. I recalled the conversation with the medical supply about the walker and put that down. Then I called the audiologist's office, told them who I was and asked if they could give me any information. The audiologist, himself, came on the line and talked with me after his secretary had pulled Mrs. Streng's chart. He said he couldn't give me much information without a signed release, but I did ask if she had a hearing aid from him.

"No," he said. "Her son and daughter both came in with her to buy the aids. They put down the deposit as required, and we ordered the hearing aids."

"How much was the deposit?"

"We require half on order and half on delivery."

"Did you fit the hearing aids?"

"Yes, we did. We have a thirty day trial, so we can make sure there is benefit from a hearing aid. If not, it's returned and, we refund all the money less a lab fee. We tried the very best, and some of the most expensive, on her. She could have benefited from less expensive models, but the children insisted they wanted only the best."

"Did she keep the hearing aids?"

"According to the billing, they were returned, and we sent her money to her."

"Do you know who returned them?"

"Not unless I get into her chart, and for that I'll need a release. I would assume she came in and brought them back like most of our patients. But I don't know for sure."

"Can you tell me, were the hearing aids useful for her?"

"Let me give you some generals regarding central hearing problems. Do you have a minute?"

"Sure," I said.

"When a person has a stroke, it is possible for the hearing loss to be a central problem. That means it becomes a processing problem. It's not damage to the ear or the hearing nerve like so many hearing losses. They may work just fine, but the individual's brain can't sort out what it's hearing.

"Because of that, we will often fit hearing aids with good success on stroke patients. It appears that an enhanced stimulus will give the brain enough power—for want of a better word—to kick it into processing. We like to follow our patients closely for just that reason. If the hearing aids work, great. It speeds recovery that much faster. If they don't, it's no good paying all that money for something to sit in a drawer."

"Do you know if they worked for her?" I asked.

"I don't. I'm not trying to evade you or keep the records classified. I really don't know. We made several return appointments; not many were kept, and it was nearing the end of the trial. We offered to extend it, but the children seemed to feel the hearing aids weren't helping their mother, so we sent Mrs. Streng's money back to her."

"To whom did you make out the check?"

"Our policy is to make it out to the patient unless

requested differently. The bookkeeper does that, so I couldn't tell you how it was made out."

"Oh, and one other thing. Did you ever meet Leticia Gallegos?"

"You mean the lady who would bring in Mrs. Streng sometimes? Really pretty woman?"

"That's the one. You remember her, then."

"Sure, who would forget her? She was a nice person, really good at handling Mrs. Streng. Did much of the talking for her. Come to think of it, I don't believe I ever heard Mrs. Streng say much. Actually, Ms. Gallegos accompanied Mrs. Streng more than her children. How's she doing?"

"She's dead." I gave him a briefly sterile synopsis of Leticia's demise.

"I'm sorry," he said. "She sure was nice."

"You've been a great help. Thank you very much," I said gratefully.

"If you get me a release, I can send this information to you. Then you might get the answers to your questions."

"I will and thanks."

TwentyFour

I HAD A FEW CALLS TO MAKE AND REPRORTS TO WRITE. As I picked up the invoices from Leticia's cereal box that were lying on my desk, the alphabet/number page reminded me of its presence. The first configuration was STE6983400212; the second was JOI19532120407; the third was NIC2973161506 and so on for about ten lines. Staring at it for the next twenty minutes didn't help to decode it, and it didn't help me get my reports done, so I 'd look at those items tonight at home.

Lunch with the gang consisted of deli sandwiches James had picked up for those of us who wanted them and delicious conversation about Jill and Kelly.

Dolly started, "Jill, are you going with a date to the Jail-Bail?"

"Maybe, I'm not sure."

"Well, what she means is she's not sure she should go with Leticia's boyfriend," said Gen. "After all, who would want to go out with an alcoholic who beats his girlfriend? I keep telling her he's just putting on a good front. She keeps standing up for him and tells me Leticia was really helping him. Can you believe that?"

As she took a breath, Jill started to interrupt, but Genevieve was faster and embarked on the same track.

"You all saw that mark on Leticia's cheek. You saw what Kelly did to her. Jill says Kelly only stayed at Leticia's house when he needed support to keep from drinking. Well, I know men, and I know no man that good looking would be able to stay out of the bed of a woman just as good looking. We all know human nature. Can you believe that bunch of garbage?"

I said quietly, "That's what he told me."

Jill, surprised, asked, "You talked to him?"

"Once, in the parking lot. He told me about..." I was going to tell them the conversation about Leticia's apartment and my experience there, but decided not to.

"About what?" Gen asked highly suspiciously.

"About Leticia helping him to dry out and recover."

"But you don't believe it, do you? He's just telling you that." Gen was incredulous.

"Why would he tell lies?" asked Dolly.

"It's so suspicious. He's always hanging around here. He was with her a lot. He was in the parking lot the night she was killed. I saw him there. Don't you think that's strange? Besides he offered to pay for her funeral. That offer has guilt all over it," Gen ragged on.

Jill got up and left, and Genny, apologizing profusely to Jill, walked all over her heels out the room.

Dolly said, "Do you think Gen's right? Do you think Kelly killed Leticia?"

James said doubtfully, "That's preposterous! Kelly's a big guy, but he seems nice enough."

"That's true, but Leticia was the most gorgeous woman I've ever seen. I bet she's that kind you read about who men would do anything for. Maybe he just got jealous or something. Maybe she was too much for him. Or maybe..." Dolly trailed off.

"Or maybe what?"

"Nothing. No, nothing."

"Maybe Jill killed her?" James asked quietly.

"No, don't say that."

"Is that what you were going to say?"

"No, no. I don't think so. No, I don't like that. This is crazy. I'm going back to my desk. I don't like thinking anyone here might hurt one of us," she exclaimed and hurried out.

James said, "I don't either. What do you think, Louisa?"

"What everybody is saying is interesting, but it doesn't seem to fit the people, does it?"

"Beats me. I'm going to work."

"Thanks for the sandwiches," I said as he went out of the lunchroom.

What did I think? They had certainly raised some interesting ideas. That they had been spoken made me realize most all of us must have worried about the same things. They had certainly crossed my mind, especially after going to the apartment with Kelly. He was there, but said he didn't come in. Jill does get a panicked look when Leticia's name is brought up. Maybe she isn't worried only about Kelly.

I wanted out of there. There was a senior citizens' residence I hadn't been to in a couple of weeks. I decided to go there and conduct a session. Maybe I could fit in a visit to Mrs. Streng.

The Patrician Towers was one of the more progressive senior citizens' residences in the county. It was built so most of the apartments in the towers had a never ending view of Mt. Diablo and its flanking peaks. Wing chairs and sofas were coordinated in colors of beige, blue and rose and placed in seating arrangements designed to relax, not only its residents, but their families as well.

There were recreational facilities to make an Olympic team envious. The food was prepared by a staff trained at culinary schools in the Bay Area. The management not only concerned itself with the health and gastronomy of its residents, it concerned itself with their mental well-being. That's where our agency came in. The management of Patrician Towers contracted with the agency to provide two one hour sessions per week for any of the residents who wished to come for drop-in support and chat groups.

I enjoyed the sessions. Many enjoyable, life-loving people came and talked about their fears of growing old, their sometimes distant families, their plans for their estates, and their physical aches and pains. So I listened and let the group members talk about whatever was bothering them. Some issues I could refer on, others only needed a word of reassurance. Today it was less intense being here than participating in what was brewing at the office.

After the group session, I went to Mrs. Streng's house. During the drive I got that stuffy feeling again, but when I arrived at the house, it went away.

"Oh, it's you," said a disappointed Percival. "I'll get my sister."

"Oh, its you," said Zoë in a much different tone than her brother. "Come back and see Mother. Mrs. Daniel, how is Ian?"

"Very fine. I saw him this morning. He's even displaying a little healthy aggression. We're keeping him for awhile at the request of the state."

"Do you think . . would it be possible … I mean, I do miss him. Could I see him, do you think?"

"I could arrange that. He'd probably enjoy it."

"Please, make it soon. He's a wonderful child."

By then we were in the sunroom. The wisteria had turned to a net of green, leafy foliage; the irises were just about gone, but summer perennials were starting to show their colors. The yellow coreopsis, the red geraniums, the ramrod straight gladiolas were getting ready for their rainbow fireworks.

"Mother, I'm going to see Ian soon," Zoë announced.

The mobile side of Mrs. Streng's face smiled.

Twenty Five

ARMEGEDDON OF SELF-CONFIDENCE FOR AN OLDER, divorced woman is walking into a social gathering unescorted. The downfall starts the day of the event, gathers momentum as the day flies by, and engulfs her by evening when it's time to dress for the occasion. Excuses for not going vacillate between getting sick (used by everybody) to telling the truth (used by nobody). People become skeptical of the first, would be solicitous of the second, so, in the end, it's easier to go. Besides, there was a job to do at the Jail-bail and not completing it would be irresponsible.

My attire for the evening was a black short cocktail dress with a plunging backline bordered with golden cutwork cascading down the neck and back like scrambled eggs, black hose because my legs had not caved in to cellulite like the rest of my body, and black and gold sequined pumps. I took a deep breath, checked in with Jill and Gen, and took my place at the ticket table to do the banking. If I had thought of it at the time of the sign-ups, I probably should have taken the first shift of tickets because I would not have had to walk through the lobby of the jail that was crowded with people. Life is a matter of opposites, and opposites come in twos, which provides life with its balance. Human beings have what must be an innate desire to have symmetry in life, and that includes relationships. As I don't date often, I appear asymmetrical to many of my friends and acquaintances. The walking data file, Gen, is one of those friends.

She said as I checked in, "I knew you didn't have a date, so I had Sid bring his friend from work. He's a stockboy at the factory. He stacks inventory. I just don't think it's safe for you to be without a man—especially late at night.

"Besides," she continued, "you have a new dress. It's just … precious. I'm so glad you didn't wear that one you always wear to these things. It was getting a little shabby."

Catching the jibe, but also the concern, I thanked her without explaining I really could take care of myself and didn't want to be bothered with the hopelessness of a blind date. I also didn't point out that I bought new dresses for most all these occasions and had not, that I could remember, worn the same one more than twice. Tonight she wore a beaded, blue, two-piece dress on her rubenesque figure. The glitter she had sprayed on her head caught the light like shiny lice moving through her hair. She had her hair tinted to match the dress, so her blue hair almost looked silver and went well with her outfit. She was waiting to be complimented, so I did.

Then I asked, "Genny, just how old is this 'stockboy'?"

"Well," she said. "Now let me think. He's older than Sid. He has to be about sixty-two or three."

"Are you telling me he's sixty-three and a *stockboy*?"

She heard the incredulity in my voice and said, "Louisa, you are so cynical. That's just his title. He has a very important job at the factory. He can't wait to meet you tonight."

"What do you mean 'tonight'?"

"Well, how could you meet him if he didn't come? I told you I had Sid bring him."

"But I thought you meant bring him to your home or something. I don't need a date, Genevieve. I'm not even staying the whole evening. I just came to do my job and uphold the pride of the agency and all that crap. I don't care to meet him."

"Of course, you do. You'll love him. He's so cute," she squealed.

Cute, at my age, worries me. If I timed it right, I could leave without her realizing it. One minute, I'd be there; the next minute, poof, I'm gone.

Surveying the lobby from the angle at which the greeters' desk sat, the turnout appeared to be another feather in Charles' fundraiser cap. The mayors and city councils of several of

Contra Costa's towns, the county sheriff, and a few hospital administrators made their appearances and even appeared to be enjoying themselves. Also arriving were several local celebrities, the people who lend their family name and finances to fundraisers such as this one.

This facility was tastefully severe. The straight lines and right angles used in construction gave a rigid cleanliness to the interior of the building. Efficiency of design melded with low maintenance in the esthetics of the building. Pale and relaxing gray pink paint provided the only decor in the lobby of the jail. Although it was designed to hold twice the number of inmates the current county jail held, predictions were it would be overcrowded within a year. As I sat there, I wondered if anyone in that future overcrowding would be able to imagine a party complete with decorations had once been held here. Black and white streamers, black and white balloons, and black and white prison striped tablecloths were the only reminders that this was a place of incarceration.

During my stint I greeted several co-workers; a few boarding home mothers; my daughter and son-in-law, who had agreed to be put in jail, some clients, including Percival and Zoë; Leticia's former and Jill's present boyfriend, Kelly, and, to my surprise, Lt. Washburn.

"Lieutenant, it's nice to see you. I had no idea you'd be coming," I said.

"I thought we'd agreed on Bob."

"Okay, Bob. You never struck me as the social fundraising type."

"I know, I know. I don't usually come to these things, but my being here will accomplish two things. It upholds the police presence in the community which can't hurt, and I thought I might observe some of the people here. I've thought about what you told me a few days ago and decided to go through some of the reports concerning Miss Gallegos' death. I couldn't find anything specific, but your mentioning the stool was something no one else had thought important enough to point out. That stool not being crushed does seem unusual. Besides that, my gut feeling keeps prodding me. That's usually an incentive for me to probe a situation a little more thoroughly."

"It's nice to see you," I said and meant it.

"Is this your job for the evening?" he asked.

"Yes."

"Great," he smiled.

Hot dog! This evening may not be so dreadful after all. After he settled in, I said, "I've found some interesting paper-work in one of Leticia's files. Perhaps on Monday, I could come and see you and bring you what I—"

"I can be in your office at 9:00 sharp," he interrupted. The speed with which he agreed to see what I had made me wonder if he had more information than he had intimated.

At events like this one people tend to arrive in gusts, then there is a lull. Our conversation was broken during these peri-ods and then continued during the lulls between ticket taking and money changing. The past few days I had determined sev-eral conversation topics if I ever had the chance to talk with him. They all seemed so impressively enlightened at the time, now they seemed like pretentious nonsense.

So I said, "Why did Lynn call you Bubba?"

Startled he said, "What?"

"Why did Lynn call you Bubba? It doesn't fit you. It's such a stereotyped name. You know, the guy with the britches that fit under the belly leaving a peek of his rear."

"Poor Bubba. The name has certainly been short shrifted of any respect. You know, it actually has a Greek origin, it comes from a word meaning boy. She called me Bubba originally because my family is from Oklahoma. They came to California in the Dust Bowl Days. She thought it was funny because her family is California history, and she got a big kick out of ruffling the complacency of her family name by marrying an Okie.

"I used to tell her Okies and Arkies were what kept California going. They were used to doing twice the amount of work on half the natural resources with one quarter of the tools available here. For them California was truly the golden state. Talk to many successful Californians and ask them where their family is from. Many of them will tell you grandpa or mom or somebody came during the dust bowl days. They weren't really welcome, but they provided a shot in the arm for California, I think."

Ask a question, get an answer. If the guy was as thorough in his work as he was in his verbal essays, no wonder he got the promotion.

He paused while his eyes indicated he was somewhere back in his memory.

"I miss Lynn. I had heard people say it's hard to watch a spouse die, and I believed them when we discovered she wasn't going to overcome the cancer. Our whole family worked hard in preparing ourselves for the time when she was gone. And it worked. It seemed we dealt with her death more easily than some families I've seen. But there's a part of the loneliness that's hard to describe, that I can't very well pinpoint. If I had to use one word to try to describe what I miss most about her, I'd say the word is friendship. But, that seems so trite and overused. We had a nice married relationship, so much so that we could go beyond that and be friends. That was probably the most valuable part of the whole marriage.

"When you called me Bubba—hearing that again—it took me back to the empty spot," he said as he looked at me and smiled almost apologetically.

In my two hour workshift, we greeted the ticketholders and watched the partiers and talked. My intentions had been to leave as soon as the shift was over, but as long as he was there, I decided I could play party animal.

So I went and gladhanded every hand I could grab. First I saw Gen and Sid.

She asked, "Who was that man at the table with you? He's kind of nice looking."

"That was Lt. Bob Washburn with the police department."

"Is that him? He called, you know. Charles told me to put him at whatever job you were doing. So I did."

"Is that true?"

"Yes, now stay here while I go get Rufus."

"The cute one?"

"Cute as a bug in a rug. And, he's such a good listener. You know, Louisa, you always feel you need men to listen to you. You always think you have such important things to say. Well, Rufus is your answer because he'll listen all day long to you. Even if it isn't that interesting. He can't wait to meet you. Now, Louisa, don't get that snotty look. You must be approachable if you want to catch a man. Stay here while I go find him."

That was my cue. As soon as she set out on her quest, I moved to anyone I knew even slightly. This was a dilemma I hadn't encountered since college dances, playing cat and mouse with a potential blind date in the hope of snaring a potentially exciting date. I happened upon Kelly, who had lit upon Jill like sonar to a submarine. Dolly and James seemed to be enjoying each other's company. There must have been more to their relationship than just filing charts. Chatting with Emily and David and meeting some of their friends was always enjoyable, but when the talk turned to their various businesses, I moved on. I even contended with the Streng siblings who were there representing their mother and were guided through the attending social register by Charles. Percival did condescend to say hello to me, but that was all. Zoë, on the other hand, wanted to stay and talk, but Charles and Percival moved her through the partying throng.

I kept mixing in the hope Gen would have a hard time finding a moving target. As I turned to head to the refreshment table set up in another room, she and Sid confronted me while Gen shrieked, "Louisa, I have him."

Just as the curtain opens upon a drama, Sid and Genny parted to reveal a very round man with a full smile on his face.

What was left of his gray hair was cut into a regulation Marine crew cut.

Sid smiled his Stan Laurel grin while Gen said, "Louisa, this is Rufus—Rufus Stubbs. Rufus, this is Louisa Daniel."

His name certainly fit.

It's hard to talk without your lips touching every once in a while, but his lips never connected as he said, "Louisa, would you like to dance?"

This man was almost a foot shorter than I was, and I had trouble envisioning dancing with a partner whose eyes were at my breast level. So I tried some conversation.

His military erectness and hairstyle led me to ask, "Were you in the service?"

"No, no. I wanted to be a Marine, but my eyesight was too bad. You wouldn't know it now because of my contacts."

That explained the bulging, blinking eyes.

"Do you have children?"

"My wife and I had fish."

"Fish?"

"We liked aquariums, no noise and no mess on the carpet," he snorted which I took to be a laugh.

I laughed at the joke and tried again, "Are you divorced?"

"No, she's dead."

"I'm sorry. Did she die recently?"

"About five years ago."

"I'm sure you still miss her."

"Sometimes."

"Yes, sometimes I miss my husband, but we're only divorced. He's not even dead."

"That's nice."

A night with Woofy was looking quantitatively better than an evening with Rufus. As I began to say "My dog is not feeling well, I'll have to. . ." Bob came and said, "I've been looking for you. You said if they played this song, you'd dance with me."

Right, I said that. I went with him gladly. Rufus pattered

over to Gen and Sid, and that was the last we saw of him. Maybe I could do field visits on Monday and not have to face Gen's wrath. Right now it was worth it.

Bob and I danced most of the evening. Although he concentrated on our time together, I could still catch his furtive glances at people who had been involved with Leticia. It didn't bother me, however, because I did the same thing. We stayed around and watched high society parading its satins and glitter in and out of various jail cells making merrier with its money as the night eroded into the first smattering of light. The more they drank, the more they spent. This year the community stood a good chance of easing many of its social ills because many programs were going to be funded with tonight's proceeds.

Twenty Six

THE POUND OF FLESH TO PAY FOR THE EARLY MORNING hour I arrived home was exorcised in a big way. My bewildered body hadn't indulged in a party like that in years, so I relegated it to the sofa ostensibly to watch television. Most of the day my brain couldn't follow even the simplest plot on any TV show, so I alternated sleeping with staring at the alphabetical/numeral patterns found in Leticia's cereal box. Only someone experienced with coding could understand the library book on cryptography I had borrowed, so that found its way to the floor with a resounding plop. Surveying the area through eyes at half-mast I saw Woofy using the book as a pillow on the floor next to the sofa. The sandwich I had made for lunch was only half eaten because my body was too tired to digest anything. The channel changer had fallen to the floor, but the lassitude in my hand prevented me from reclaiming it and banishing the infomercial on cosmetics.

That was Saturday. Sunday was scheduled to be active, so I couldn't indulge myself as I had the day before.I picked up JoJo and Lulie early because David and Emily were off to a reception for some honoree connected with David's business. The girls had decided we would go to Marine World, so off we drove to the land of bubble gum colors and sugar-grease junk food.

We walked the circuit, ate the junk, and, by afternoon, JoJo thought it would be nice to spend the night at Grandma and Woofy's house. I embraced the idea, but we needed to call their parents. We tramped over to a pay phone. Marine World is in a different county and area code than Pleasant Creek. The Bay Area has been hacked into as many area and

135

zip codes as royal necks were hacked from bodies in the French Revolution, so making a phone call to Emily and David was not merely a matter of inserting a couple coins and dialing their number. Rather, it was a matter of long distance and calling cards to reach them.

I'd like to think that I would have logically deduced the answer if I hadn't had such an exhilarating evening Friday night because it was such a simple solution not to have figured it out before. The cryptographical solution to Leticia's code was right there on the phone. The prefix on the payphone was the same as one of the number patterns on Leticia's list of codes. I copied it down to make sure while I talked to David and got his okay for the girls to stay with me.

JoJo and I then spent the rest of the afternoon trying to explain to Lulie why we couldn't find an alligator for her to pet like in her storybook. I let JoJo do most of the talking because my mind wouldn't tuck away the number puzzle and possible solution.

I practically dragged Woofy around the block. He knew I was in a hurry to get to work, so he, thankfully, finished his business quickly. Not only did I have to get JoJo and Lulie home, I also wanted to get to work soon, so I could justify leaving in the early afternoon and spend the evening in the library looking up phone numbers. I also needed to drop my car off for the smog check, and the library and gas station were within walking distance of each other. With luck the main branch would have a Criss-Cross directory, and I could find out the names belonging to the numbers. Based upon the prefix at Marine World, a reexamination of the numbers on Leticia's list indicated the phone number consisted of the first seven digits. I still didn't know what the letters were, nor did I know the last three digits.

There was a message on my desk when I arrived saying that Lt. Washburn would not be in today and would call to reschedule. I had just missed the call, and I probably wouldn't be in the rest of the day to take his return call.

People at the office were quieter nowadays. We stayed in our offices more. There was less coffee klatching, and instead of hooking up in the hallways and talking, we merely nodded to each other in passing. Some of the sobriety was the letdown of the Jail-Bail being over. As we had guessed Friday night, the fiscal outcome was going to be highly beneficial for the community agencies, but there was no tangible goal for the staff to work toward now. And, Leticia's death and funeral created much of the sobriety. The funeral was a lukewarm memorial at the mortuary with no reception afterward. Nobody had much to say because nobody knew her well enough to say much. Such a diluted celebration of a life completed was only depressing.

I had to hand it to Genevieve, however, because she did attempt to brighten the days with her haircolor. The color for this week was red, not chestnut or auburn, red as in crayon.

"Louisa," she sang out.

"Genevieve," I lilted.

"You weren't nice to Rufus."

"Sure I was, we talked about his pets."

"He left early."

"He looked tired. Maybe he had a hard day stocking inventory."

"Louisa, I don't know why I try so hard with you. You are the most ungrateful woman I know." There was a pause. "Actually, Leticia was probably the most ungrateful. But you're right up there with her. I don't know if I shall ever get you a date again. You always chase them away."

She changed the direction of the repartee. "Why did you dance all the time with that policeman?"

"He asked me."

"The whole night?"

"The whole night."

"Well?"

"Well, what?"

"Don't you have something to tell me?"

"About what?"

"Louisa," she said warningly. "About Friday night and that Washburn fellow."

"I worked the desk with him, I danced with him, I went home late. Satisfied?"

"Louisa, you are impossible! Tell me what happened. No one ever dances with you that much. You ditched Rufus and went off with that fellow."

"I told you what happened, and I didn't ditch Rufus. He left when Bob Washburn asked me to dance."

"I'm going to find Jill," she snorted.

Good. I'm going to finish my lunch and find the library.

I checked out with Dolly, drove into the gas station, and asked the attendant if he could check my smog device and give me a certificate.

"Sure," he said.

"Can I get the car back in a couple hours? I'll just be at the library," I asked.

"No problem."

The reference librarian gave me the Criss-Cross directories, but he only had Contra Costa and Alameda counties. He said he had no other Bay Area counties at that branch, so I'd have to go to the main libraries in those counties if I wanted the rest of the Bay Area. But it was a start, so I plowed through. Only one of the numbers listed was in the directory, and it was in Alameda County. The number belonged to a John Villarreal. The code Leticia had used for that number began with the three letters JOH, so I assumed the first three letters of her code were the beginning of a name.

I couldn't be certain, however, because the library didn't have all the Criss-Crosses, but did have the phone directories for major cities in the nation. Checking the San

Francisco and San Jose directories showed the majority of the telephone prefixes to be in those areas. The Marin county directory yielded the remainder.

TwentySeven

"I CAME TO PICK UP MY CAR. I"M MRS. DANIEL," I SAID TO the lady at the cashier's window.

"Leon wants to talk to you."

"Which one is Leon?"

"Your car is parked around the side—Oh, here's Leon."

"This your car?" said Leon, a man in a starched white shirt who had thistle eyebrows.

"Yes, it is."

He took a stance of moderate anguish when he put his hand to his neck, and the thistles dropped in scrutiny of my car and me.

"You got a problem."

"Uh-oh."

"The smog device seems okay, but we're getting a high reading of CO in your exhaust."

"CO?"

"Carbon monoxide. You been sleepy in the car? You drive with your windows open?"

"The weather's been pretty nice. I drive with my windows open a lot. I like the natural cool. I don't drive with them closed, but I don't … Oh, you're right. I did notice that. I got sleepy when I drove out from East County. I was worried about not having gas, but now I remember. That was it. I remember. Then there was another time, but it was a short trip. It wasn't as bad."

"We oughta get your permission, but couldn't find you at the library. Gail, the cashier, tried to call.

"Anyway, we had some time, so we poked around a bit. You got a hole in your muffler. That may be where the CO is getting in."

"Guess I hit a rock or something?"

"No," he said thoughtfully. "No, I don't think that's it. The hole's too neat. Someone got under there with a big nail or something and punched it through with a hammer. And, there's a long tube connected. It goes all the way through the floor in your back seat. C'mere, I'll show you."

Leon guided me to my car. He opened the driver's door and pulled the seat back forward. "If you look real close—See how the nap is kinda rough?"

He was right. The only time I spend in the back seat of my car is when I vacuum the rug at the car wash, and the hole was small enough that I very likely would never have seen it. If I had, I might figure one of the children had pulled it with a toy.

"We can patch the muffler here. You might wanna wait and let us do it now."

I must have looked as distressed as I felt because he said with a nervous chuckle, "Everyone's got enemies."

Immediately after the Woofer's walk, I started calling Leticia's list. We made it a short walk, not only because I wanted to get through the list, but also I didn't want to send thoughts careening around my head. I was scared and concerned my fear would escalate to terror. I didn't want to think about how Leticia, the bump at the condo, and the hole in my muffler were related—not yet, anyway.

John Villarreal had an answering machine. I hung up because I didn't want to leave my phone number with someone I didn't know.

A live voice answered the next call with, "Lee residence."

It seemed wiser to keep it professional, so I identified myself with, "This is Louisa Daniel with the Community Action Group, a social work agency. I'm trying to obtain information about a person named Leticia Gallegos. Would you be able to help me?"

"I know no one by that name," she said.

"Is there anyone in your household who would, do you think?"

"I'm sorry, who did you say you were?" she asked suspiciously.

I repeated my opening paragraph, but I also said, "If I leave you my number, would you please call me if you think of anyone. Or would you please ask anyone in your household if they know the name? I would very much appreciate it."

"I guess so," she said reluctantly and hung up before I could say anything else.

The next call answered "Law offices."

Not having a name, I didn't know how to respond, so I said, "Which offices?"

"These are the offices of Harkin, Hazbin, Hutchings and Azolah," said an overly affected, impatient voice.

"I'm afraid I have the wrong number." She hung up without saying good bye.

It went like that for the next four calls. Three were answering machine messages; one so decadently suggestive I fleetingly questioned the interpretation of free speech. I didn't leave return messages. There was one lady who hung up on me as soon as I mentioned Leticia's name. I tried calling back, but she slammed down the receiver as soon as she heard my voice. The third try to that number was a busy signal. Leticia's name obviously had an effect on her. She was annoyed enough to make me think Leticia must have done a number on her, too.

Two more calls to go. The first of those was answered by a man's deep voice. I opened with the same spiel as with the only other live male voice I had encountered.

"Look, lady, you can't call me here and talk about this. This is my house," he sounded desperately nervous.

"This is the only number I have."

"Where did you get it?"

"From a list I found in Leticia's house."

"She said she didn't keep lists. It was all private, she said. I never gave her this number. You can't have my name."

"But I do."

"Look, give me your number. I'll call you back. Just don't call back here."

"All right. But if I don't hear from you in two days, I'll call you again."

"Okay, okay."

"There's one thing you need to know. She's dead, you can't get hold of her."

There was a considerable silence. Then a click.

I starred that number and made a note to call back in two days. I reached out to call the last number, but left my hand on the receiver because an awareness started coalescing. I didn't want that for Leticia; I hoped it wasn't so, but it sure would explain some things.

Twenty Eight

THE INTEROFFICE PHONE RANG.

"Mrs. Streng's on line three," said Dolly. "I thought you told me she couldn't talk."

"She can't. It must be *Miss* Streng, her daughter."

"Oh. You're probably right."

"Hello, Miss Streng. How are you doing? Is everything all right?"

"There's no change in Mother. I called for two reasons. I talked with Percival about the walker, and he said he didn't know anything about it. Could Leticia have ordered it, do you think?"

"Could be. She didn't have any note about it in her file, though."

"I don't guess we'll ever need it. Mother just gets worse every day. Both the physical and occupational therapists are starting to talk about dismissing her for lack of progress. They feel it's ridiculous to waste our money, the insurance company's money, and their time."

"That's certainly decisive."

"Percival and I feel they should hang in there just a little longer. Could you call them with some encouragement to do so?"

"I'll be glad to. What's the other thing?"

She was hesitant, she stuttered around a bit, but finally said, "I'd like to adopt Ian."

She started explaining rapidly, "I know it sounds unusual. I've thought about it very much. I'm thinking about leaving my job or doing it part time. I've been thinking about it ever since Mother's stroke. I have no plans to marry, but I know there are many single people who have children. I'll be as accommodating as I can."

"Wait, Zoë." I interrupted. "That case hasn't been finalized yet. The parents haven't said definitely what their plans are, and, even if they release their baby for adoption, he may have physical, emotional, or learning problems, or all of those. None of us knows what kind of neglect he's undergone and what long term effects he may suffer."

"I don't care. I want him for my own."

"Let's make a time to talk. We need to go through this in great detail."

"I'll bring my attorney. He'll get the adoption through."

"Zoë, wait. You don't have to involve an attorney yet. I'll help you as much as I can. I'd like to see Ian have a good home, too. Right now, I want to answer any questions you have and get some preliminary information from you. I'm not telling you you can't adopt. I'm telling you there are some situations we have to understand before we get started, that's all."

"Oh, I know you're right. But I really want that baby."

"Have you talked to Percival about this?"

"No, and he doesn't need to know. This is my decision. Nothing in this decision should affect him. I think he's going to like the idea of having a little boy who looks so much like him around. I haven't done much in my life without his guidance, so I want this to be a surprise. He'll be so proud of me when he realizes what I've done on my own."

We made an appointment, and I hustled off to Charles to get an update on Ian's status.

When I got a fix on Charles' movements for the day from Dolly, I was able to trap some time with him and tell him there was a person who was interested in adopting Ian. He said the final decree had not been decided because the parents didn't keep the last scheduled court date.

"Apparently the mother is having second thoughts about letting go of the baby. She's concerned he won't be loved," he said as he rolled his eyes.

"If the judge is made aware there is someone who

wants to and can care for him, perhaps it would help influence the parents," I pointed out.

"Courts don't like to separate children from natural parents, you know that. That's probably a carry-over from cave law and survival. It's difficult to try to second guess any family law judge. The court is trying to do what's best for the child, and there are at least two sides of the story, maybe more if grandparents or some other family member or agency becomes involved. You've been through this, you know how it works—or doesn't—as the case may be."

"You're right, but I wanted you to know. It would be nice to see Ian get a boost in life," I said as I started to leave his office. I couldn't escape before he asked the question I had been so carefully avoiding.

"Who are the prospective parents, Louisa?"

"I'll let you know if it gets any further. It's still in the talking stage right now."

"Louisa, who is it?"

"Charles, you don't need to know right away." Wrong thing to say. It was taking the finger out of the dike to unleash a torrent of words.

"Louisa, you cannot let Zoë Streng adopt that baby! She has no business with a child. He has terrific needs. She has a career. Percival is so worried about his mother, especially when that child is around her. Zoë has to think of the effect on her family."

"I haven't met with her yet. I can't say she's thought this out completely," I tried to calm him.

That night, there was a message on my answering machine to call Bob Washburn. Thinking he had some new ideas about Leticia, I returned his call and was pleasantly—no excitedly—surprised when he asked if we could meet for dinner tomorrow night. We made the arrangements, and I didn't think of much else that evening.

We had settled on a restaurant specializing in California cuisine, a catch all term for any ethnic food and many fresh and *al dente* vegetables mixed in a way to match the chef's mood that day.

"How's the office?" Bob asked.

"A little dreary and edgy. The staff doesn't feel the circumstances of Leticia's death are resolved. They're speculating on who could have killed her."

"What do they say?"

I told him their conjectures. Then he asked, "How are you doing?"

"I'm okay. No, I'm almost okay." I told him about Leticia's apartment and my knockout, and I told him about the carbon monoxide.

After digesting that and our salads, we started talking about our kids. It was a cautiously non-intimidating start, but we quickly took the conversation to our individual lives. It must have been a relaxing evening for both of us because it didn't seem that long until the waiters were loitering around the restaurant and loudly putting away dishes as cues for us to leave.

As Bob walked me to my car, he said, "You should probably keep a tight schedule and review it with Emily."

"I can't do that. My job isn't a nine to five sit down job. I move constantly."

"I know, but please try," he said as we faced each other. "Because, you know, it would be a shame to not have another night out together."

"Yes, it sure would," I mumbled as he came closer to me.

A nice, long kiss, a short good-bye and our lovely evening came to an end.

Twenty Nine

ZOË'S PHONE CALL PIQUED MY CURIOSITY, SO IT SEEMED prudent to pay the family a visit. Zoë, however, was not available, Percival informed me when he answered the door.

"You may go back to see Mother. I assume that's why you're here," he said pompously. He may have looked like the all-American boy, but he sure acted like the all-American brat.

I slowly walked through the living room admiring the antiques and *objets d'art*, across the atrium and into the sun porch. Mrs. Streng's dignity had been ebbing so that now she looked as dilapidated as a newspaper left in the rain. Her depression increased her fragility and made her seem almost tiny. What a change from the charming benevolence and courtesy she had exhibited before. Her head hung forward, and she didn't look up when I said hello. I went to the bed, put my hand under her chin to raise her face and said hello again. She briefly looked at me and started to drop her chin, which I still held. She closed her eyes. I talked to her quietly and told her I was there to see her family, that Zoë missed Ian, that she wanted to see him more. I mentioned that even though Leticia was assigned Ian, she didn't have a chance to meet him. With that last statement, Mrs. Streng's body jerked. Her eyes startled open, and she had a look of alarm in them. My surprise at that reaction made me drop her chin, but her head stayed up. Her lips made sporadic movements like she would tell me something, if she could talk. Mewling sounds and some quiet grunts were the only audibles she made. Zoë and Percival walked in, and Mrs. Streng's head dropped to her chest.

Percival said, "I thought you'd be gone by now."

Zoë said, "Now, Percival", and then to me, "How are you, Mrs. Daniel?"

"I'm fine. Tell me, has your mother seen her physician?"
Zoë stiffened, and Percival left the room.

"No. I can't get her to go. She raises a fuss and curls up like a child. She doesn't look well, does she?"

"No, she doesn't." Again, I went to Mrs. Streng and asked if I could take her to the doctor. No head raised; there was no answer. I reached for her hand and asked again.

"I'll take you back to Dr. Cannaughton if you'd like to see her," I cajoled. "Please let me take you."

She squeezed my hand, and I asked her if that meant I could take her. She nodded yes slightly, and I went to the phone to make the arrangements. Dr. Cannaughton was out of town, so we set up a time for later in the week.

Zoë started talking about Ian. I gave her the information Charles had shared with me and some of the concerns he had for the whole situation. She had logical answers for all the issues I raised, but we reconfirmed our appointment. As I left mother and daughter, I was heartened not only by Zoë's responses to the potential adoption of Ian, but also by Mrs. Streng's promise to see her physician.

Thirty

He CALLED THAT EVENING, OUT OF BREATH.

"This is the fellah you called …You know, two days ago …I told you I couldn't talk to you on the phone. I forget your name … You called about Leticia …Remember?"

"I remember. Can you talk for a few minutes?"

"I think so … My wife is out playing poker. She can't know this, so you have to keep this quiet … If you tell anyone I called, I'll deny it … What did you say about Leticia being dead?"

I gave him sketchy details of the accident. Then I asked, "How do you know her?"

His panting quit as he started describing Leticia. "She was a looker. She could charm a snake out of his skin. She told the funniest stories, and she could make the party."

If she hadn't had an unusual name, I might have thought we got our Leticias mixed up.

"Beg your pardon?"

"Are you part of her business?"

"Yes, I worked with her."

"Do you charge the same rates?"

"I'm sure we do. We do similar jobs."

"You as good looking as her?"

"No, she was younger and much more glamorous."

"That's okay. You don't have to be a beauty. Just dress great. Are you as good at the other stuff?"

"Other stuff?"

"Yeah, you know. Afterward."

"You mean like follow-ups."

"I guess so. Well, I don't know. I always had to pay for follow-ups because that was a new appointment. I guess you could call them follow-ups," he continued.

"Oh, you were billed on an hourly basis?"

"No, hell, I paid cash—flat rate."

"Did you give it to Dolly?"

"Is Dolly another one of you. I'll be goddamned. Leticia told me she had a service. I thought she was blowing smoke up my ass. Just making herself look good. Man, that's good to know about Dolly. I got friends who might need her. Is she as good as Leticia?"

"I suppose so; she's the receptionist, and she's always seemed competent to me."

"You mean you're in a building? You have an office? I thought those were illegal. Hot damn, this is great news! Where is it?"

"The business is in Pleasant Creek. It's on Main near the Mall."

"What are the hours?"

"Nine to five. Monday through Friday. Nine to noon on Saturday."

"Nine at night to five in the morning? How do you get away with that? Shit, weekends would be your busiest times. You'd have customers comin' out your ass. You must be paying off somebody in city hall, right?"

"What are you talking about? We are open regular business hours. We do semi-private and public social work. Leticia was a caseworker like I am."

"No, lady, Leticia had an escort service."

"An escort service?"

"Yeah, she had an escort service. But, I thought it was just her. Hell, I didn't know she had gals working for her. She'd meet me. I just used her about three weeks ago. I'd take her out, and we'd go to a hotel. I even had her entertain some of guys from the out of town offices. They always asked for her. One of the best in the business. Damn, she was good. If you could do it like she could, I've got the customers for you."

The day that had gone so swimmingly just drowned.

Perhaps in an inner recess of my mind, I had had an inkling of how Leticia moonlighted, literally as it turns out. There were enough clues: the new and expensive clothes every season, her household furnishings, the brusque rudeness and her unabashed glamour, keeping odd hours, even the bruise. Do what you enjoy and the money will follow. In many ways her jobs jived with her life. Manipulation was her forte, and she seemed to enjoy it. She did it often for her clients, and she was always manipulating one of her co-workers. She played the role and then took the money. With us she discovered the problem and then took our time and energy.

No matter how Leticia was with us, I had always felt she really cared for her clients; they were her anchors to reality. I never had the idea she was working her wiles on them for the purpose of playing some game. After the evening's call, I wasn't so sure.

ThirtyOne

"Did you get Miss Steng to eliminate the idea of adopting the unadoptable?" asked Charles when he saw me in the hallway. He wore a taupe suit, jade green pin-striped shirt and a tie with a forest motif that looked like you could walk in and have a picnic. If men could look ravishing, he would.

"You mean Ian?"

"No, that's not his name. I'm talking about the child who was left in the crib by his parents."

"That's the one. Mrs. Chu decided he looked more like Ian."

"Ian who?"

"I don't know, Charles. That's how she operates. She decides what name fits each child's personality."

"I wish she wouldn't do that," he muttered. "It confuses me. So, did you dissuade Miss Streng?"

"No, but I talked with her. She's already thought out solutions to the problems you foresee. Do you want to meet with us when she comes in?"

"Perhaps, I'd better. Check with Dolly and see if my schedule will allow it," he said as I stepped into my office.

I called Emily and gave her a rundown of my schedule to the best of my prediction for the next couple of days.

"Why are you doing this?" she asked.

"Doing what?"

"Giving me your schedule when I can barely keep track of my own?"

"Bob Washburn thought it might be a good idea."

"And?"

"And so I'm giving you my schedule."

"Mother, what's going on?"

"Let me see. Right now I have just arrived at the office, and I'm calling you first thing."

"On time as usual, I see. Tell me what's happening, or I'll call him."

"Emily, I got bumped on the head at Leticia's, and someone fixed my car so it would put out carbon monoxide poisoning while I was driving."

Emily paused before she said, "Come on, Mom. What are you talking about? Why were you at Leticia's? She's dead. What's going on?"

"Nothing, Emily. I'm just giving you my schedule, that's all. Everything's fine."

"No, there're things you're not telling me. Are you afraid?"

"Of course not, why should I be afraid?" I laughed.

"You're lying."

"What do you mean?"

"You can't even fake a carefree laugh. When are you leaving work tonight?"

"I'm not sure. I've got some cases to update. Depends on how long that takes."

"Here's what I want you to do. Go get Woofy and come here for dinner. You might consider staying with us for the next few days or so. At least, until this whatever you're dealing with blows over."

"Oh, Emily, don't be ridiculous. I can handle this."

"I'm not being ridiculous. And, don't tell me you can handle this by yourself. You need help. Be here tonight with your dog, understand?"

"Yes, I guess so."

After both of us calmed down, I gave Emily my schedule and checked in with Dolly. We reappointed Zoë's time, so Charles could attend the meeting. By talking with her personally, he would realize she would probably make a stable mother for Ian.

Eating in the lunchroom was like being in a library. If anyone talked, it was in whispers. Most had documents or books to read, so they could munch with their heads down and not look at any co-workers. The scene could really have been shaken up if I told them about Leticia's other job. That jolt of gossip could inflame the whole office, and Genevieve would be right in the middle fanning the flames into a roaring inferno. But Leticia's memory didn't deserve that, so I kept quiet.

ThirtyTwo

I DIDN'T THINK THE PAPERWORK WOULD TAKE AS LONG as it did, so I didn't leave the agency until around 8:00 that evening. The hallway felt eerie because it was so dark with all but the security lights off and the doors to the offices shut for the night. At the end of the hall was a light in Charles' office, so I thought I'd pop in to say goodnight to Betty. She'd often stay later than the rest of us to set up the next day.

"Have a nice evening, Betty," I said to a neatly organized but empty desk. Betty was nowhere to be found in the office.

"Louisa, come in here. Please," Charles said.

Uh-oh, I thought as I waddled into his office loaded with my briefcase, purse, empty lunch bag and sweater.

"Night, Charles," I said as I poked my head in his inner office "Don't you want to wrap it up?" I asked. "You've probably been here longer than I have today, and you haven't even begun to clear your desk for the evening. Even Betty has left."

Ignoring my hints, he asked, "Would you mind taking a few minutes to discuss Zoë and this adoption she thinks she wants? I need to know where she got this hare-brained idea."

"Truly, Charles, I have no idea where she got it. It was not mine." I set down my many containers on one of the chairs.

"Her brother is quite annoyed she is even contemplating such an idea."

A pause while what he just said registered. "Her brother? How does Percival know?"

He jerked slightly and said, "Well, obviously, she told him."

"No, Charles, obviously she didn't tell him. That was something she was very explicit about. No one was to know. She wants to adopt Ian, but I had talked her into meeting here and going through this methodically. I wanted to do that, so she could see what she was going to let herself in for. I thought that by doing that, we could buy some time and make the best of the situation. Who told him, Charles? Who told him about the baby?" I repeated, but his answer would be superfluous because I knew. I sank into the chair and absently shoved my stuff to the floor. My mind replayed the scene at the Jail-Bail when I met Charles hanging on to Percival and Zoë while he introduced them to various attendees. And the more I thought about it, the more I realized he was literally hanging onto them, monopolizing them the whole evening. It's funny how a sudden flash of knowledge isn't a surprise. It seems like it should be, but it isn't because the brain had reasoned it out without the individual being aware the situation was explained. The surprise is not the solution to the puzzle; the surprise is the time lag in not recognizing it.

"You were the one, weren't you, Charles? Leticia found out and told you, didn't she? I thought it was Zoë or Percival, but I couldn't figure out how they could get her in here."

He looked at me with a puzzled expression, "What are you talking about, Louisa?"

"How did you make the cabinet fall on her?" I asked it quietly because I really didn't want to go there.

"We're talking about Zoë and the adoption, Louisa. I have no idea what you are even saying," he said in his most prickly manner.

After a pause while I realized what I had said and replayed the conclusion in my head, I said, "Why did it have to be you? Oh, Charles, why?"

Charles sat upright and stood stock-still, shoulders straight back, face blank, eyes looking at me and not focusing.

"I knocked her out and laid her on the floor. Charles talked about the loose bolt. He had only to grab the crowbar in my car and pry the thing, and, she was no problem anymore," said the rough voice from the outer office. Before I saw the voice, I remembered a picture in the hallway of memories at the

Strengs' home. Percival and Charles and some buddies, twenty five years ago at where? Boarding school? College? Not expecting Charles to be in Percival's sphere made him unrecognizable as a young man to me, but it was obvious now because Charles has aged very little. I never saw it when I was looking directly at it, and, now, here it was, a blatantly terrifying connection. Laying my head against the wall behind my chair, I closed my eyes against what I knew was coming.

Pieces of thoughts were connecting behind my closed eyes like children's building blocks to form a story I didn't want to hear. New twists and ramifications of phrases I had heard and episodes I had seen were linking up, breaking apart and linking up again with blurring speed. The invoices, the walker, Percival and Charles at boarding school, Mrs. Streng in her unaware huddle, Charles' ranting about the baby and my work habits. Because all those strings of unraveled speculations took me away from Charles' office, I didn't see Percival come up to Charles and put his arm around him. When I opened my eyes I did see Charles give Percival a kiss on the cheek and snuggle in closer to him.

And now I knew why.

Thirty Three

"I ONLY CALLED YOU IN HERE TO DISMISS YOU FROM THE Steng case," said Charles apologetically. "Percival had told me to relieve you, to get you out of his mother's life. You were suppose to quit seeing Mrs. Streng. That's all."

I opened my mouth to ask a question, but the words refused to come forth. On the next try the voice exuded slowly out of my throat, and I asked, "What about Zoë? Does she want me to quit seeing her mother?"

With bombastic chauvinism Percival said, "She'll do anything I tell her to do. After all, I am her big brother."

"Except adopt Ian."

Grim annoyance jumped across his face, and then he lunged toward my chair. I ducked as he shouted, "You bitch, if you had never brought that kid to the house and told her all that maudlin sap about him, she never would have thought she could even do it. You are wrecking my world. I need to kill you."

"Kill her? What do you mean kill her?" Charles asked as shocked as I was.

"You're just as stupid as she is," exploded Percival. "Surely, you don't think we can just let her go. She knows as much as Leticia did. She's had her nose in my business since she met me."

"But," Charles stammered, "you don't know she knows anything." Turning to me, he asked, "You don't know anything, do you, Louisa? You don't know what Percival has done?"

I swallowed hard enough that all of us could hear my gulp, and I didn't answer to the negative fast enough to be believable. Percival wasn't going to believe anything from me. There are some things to be said for stalling. Besides, if I'm late for everything else, why not be late for dying?

"I know, Charles. The audiologist put me on to it. If you're going to kill me, at least, let me see if I've got it right."

Percival shrugged his shoulders and said, " Let the old broad figure it out. She thinks she's so smart. Just like Mother. She thought she was so smart until I showed her who was smarter—and stronger. These old hags. They get to be about forty-five, and they lose it all. Stupid bitches, all of them. I won't let Zoë get that way."

"She thought you were great when she was growing up," I said.

"I know, and I really played her for everything I could use her for. I made her go and ask Father and Mother for favors for me, and the little shit did it. She was so stupid. She still is. Look at how wonderful she thinks I am. I make her think she has the ideas about taking care of Mother and play her like a fiddle."

"You mean you never liked her?"

"No, she was an interruption in my life. I didn't need her; that's why I stayed at school. One look at my stepfather when I came home after she was born, and I knew his adoration for me was over. He still acted like I was special, but he did it more for Mother's sake. That way, he kept her happy. Everyone always made sure Mother was happy. But did they ever make sure I was? Charles, did they?"

Charles simpered in answer, "I always tried to, Percival."

"Yeah, yeah, yeah. You try, sometimes you succeed."

"But, you said I made you happy. You just told me that last night. You said it, Percival."

"Okay, stupid ass. Tell us how you figured everything." Although he was looking at Charles, Percival was talking to me, and I decided to play Scheherazad and drag this out as long as I could. Fear was starting to erode any clearheadedness I had, and I really didn't know how long I could sound coherent. My heart was doing a double-time, heavy-sounding thump, and sweat was beginning to accumulate in my armpits.

"Leticia had some invoices left in your mother's file, and she had written my name and phone number on the back of one of them. She called me to come and meet her. I went to her place, but she received a call and then wouldn't talk to me. It was you who called, Percival. She was killed two days after that. Guess you said you'd work some deal with her. Or, did you get her to come to see you to blackmail her?"

"Blackmail her?" Charles was puzzled as he repeated, "Why would you do that?"

Eyes squinting hatred, Percival's face was a mottled mask of fury as he screamed at Charles, "You moronic planner! You said you had it all worked out!"

"Percival, relax. She's disorganized. You're losing control. We can handle this…" Charles sputtered.

"No, *we* can't handle this, but I can. You idiot!"

Percival turned to me. "Blackmail? That wouldn't scare her. She wasn't the type to be blackmailed. Some deal." He laughed with irony. "Blackmail her? No, in fact, I offered her more money to leave Mother's case. She said she had all the money she needed. She told me to stay away from Mother and Zoë. She said if I didn't leave Mother alone, she would go to the insurance companies who would start fraud investigations against me. What a stupid bargain! She could have taken the money. Then she would have lived a little longer until I could figure out how to get rid of every trace of her. I told Charles to do it, but he's been such a moron about the whole thing. He has this idea about human life being important. I say, if something's in the way, just get rid of it.

"You stupid wimp," he directed the last statement at Charles who sat against a wall with uncertainty and anguish on his face.

I spoke up. "So Charles assigned me the case and didn't think I'd do much with it. But, to make sure, he kept belaboring my work habits in an attempt to make me feel insecure and keep me from seeing your family. Ian kept bringing me back to your home because I knew how much the two women liked having him around. That and Dr. Cannaughton. She talked about how your mother should be doing better. No one could figure out how come your mother was regressing when she should have been getting better."

"I made sure she didn't get all of her medicine. I never told Zoë about most of her rehab appointments, so she never took Mother to them. It was so simple. She'll die soon. She complained about headaches before her stroke, and I told her it was probably flu or allergies. She had the stroke after I hit her one day."

"You hit your mother?" I said in amazement.

"Yeah, like this." He said it as he hauled his fist back and punched my face hard. Like a cartoon character, my neck stretched to a limit farther than I thought capable; my cortex slapped against my skull, and, in that instant, I knew who had hit me at Leticia's house because the feeling was the same. The warm, salty blood where my teeth connected with my inside lip choked off anything I might have said.

I didn't pass out this time, so I saw Charles spill out of his corner and try to help me. He was held back by Percival who said, "What are you doing? She's just a scheming bitch."

To me he smugly said, "That's how I hit her, only she didn't get up, so I left her lying there. After a few hours I went back to the room hoping she had died. If she had died, I would have inherited my correct portion of my stepfather's estate. Zoë got most of it, and I would finally have Mother's share, so we'd be even. But I had to make sure I could get all the estate. The stroke wasn't in my plans because I had to see the will, and the trustees always put me off. I needed more time, so I went back and got an ambulance for her. Damn women! Always ruining my life! Daddy always treated me like we were both his kids until he died. Then he gave Zoë more than me because Mother plotted against me for Zoë when I was at school."

Percival's violating blow did help displace some of my fear with anger that, under the circumstance, was probably a healthier emotion. I reached into the pocket of my skirt and took out a tissue to soak up the blood.

"You didn't inherit it, so you stole it."

"Tie her up, and get something to mop up that blood," he shouted at Charles who went looking for rags and ropes.

Charles did the mopping while Percival did the tying. Maybe if it had been the other way around, I could have gotten out of the ropes because Charles was uncomfortable and anxiously pleading with his eyes for something of me. Quiet? Good behavior? Forgiveness?

"You bet I took the money. It was mine, and it was so easy. I just had the doctors and therapists make out the bills before the services, so I could send them to the trustees who could bill insurance or pay them out of the trust. Then I returned the item or discontinued the services and got the money back. Nobody questioned me because I had them mail the check to my address. Piece of cake. Zoë and Mother will never have any idea of the items I've ordered for Mother."

It looked as though Percival was getting ready to adjourn our gathering, and I was running out of stall tactics. I caught at one of the many questions racing through my head and said, "You were the one at Leticia's condo."

"Give the gal a point. Yes. I needed to know what she had written down about Mother because Charles gave the file to you before I could read it. The dumb shit! I used the keys from her purse I got the night of her accident. It was so easy!"

"But you didn't find anything, did you?"

"No," he said dejectedly.

"And my muffler?" I was desperate to think of something else to talk about.

He said, "How come you didn't die? Oh, hell, it doesn't matter. You will now."

"Come on, Charles, we'll take her up to Marin and throw her off a cliff."

Charles whined, "Percival, you can't do that. It's so barbaric."

Percival yanked me up out of the chair, and when I complained he was hurting me, he looked at me with a nasty grin and said, "Good."

Thirty Four

IT'S NOT VERY OFTEN I GET TO RIDE IN A LUXURY CAR, even if it is in the trunk with the spare tire and various tools as my traveling companions. If I got out of this one, I could testify to the smooth ride of the Lincoln Town Car. The mellifluous hum of the engine and the softness in my head would have been sleep inducing, except the ropes were so taut, my hands were starting to hurt and throb.

A sweat worked up doing an intense power walk has a way of oiling the brain for productive thought, but the sweat of fear has a way of rusting the brain for no thought. I was lying in a sweat bath that had immobilized not only my brain, but my body as well, like the Tin-man in The Wizard of Oz. Try as hard as I could, I couldn't begin to see a solution to the situation. As soon as I'd clutch at an idea, it would tumble away from me. The more I tried to clutch it, the faster it tumbled. The faster it tumbled, the more fearful I became. And the more fearful I became the more shackled I became. Trying to adjust my position, so I could untorque myself, I turned only to have the folds of my skirt turn with me and let me lie on the contents of my pocket. The position was more comfortable for the muscles of my back, but now the small items in my pocket were digging into it. I had held angry frustration back until images of the family came before me, and then the tears started. It took me back to anger, however, when the salty tears hit my swollen lip, so I quit feeling sorry for myself. David was the last of the images to flash in my mind. But that was also a eureka moment. A few years ago just in time for Christmas presents, David had discovered mini Swiss army knives. In my pocket and currently giving me a princess and the pea sized backache was the key ring containing the very small knife and scissors. It also had a very small nail file, but I didn't think that was going to do much for my situation. I wasn't even sure about the minute scissors and knife, but it was a hope that made it worth a try. The only difficulty was rewrapping my skirt in a way to allow me to retrieve the knife. That and the time element. This skirt's waist was elastic to allow a bit more room for our older ladies' fuller figures, so it twisted relatively easily.

Percival had mentioned Marin county and a cliff which must be where we were headed. If he were headed to northern Marin, which would be less densely populated than the opposite end near San Francisco, he would take the Richmond-San Rafael Bridge and head up 101 or, and this was a thought that made me whittle the ropes even faster, Highway 1. Highway 1 is the Bonneville Salt Flats for every recreational vehicle driver west of the Rockies. If an RV operator could negotiate the swerves and curves of that two lane eighth wonder of the world, his mettle was tested and won. If an impatient Percival links up behind an RV on Highway 1, he's liable to stop his car and not care over what cliff I get the heave-ho. Time could be very short.

But it wasn't. Because I couldn't see the glowing hands on my watch, I couldn't know how long the drive had been, although it seemed we should be out of Marin County. Theoretically, they could travel about four hours to make it past Ft. Bragg and still get home before dawn. Headlands and precipices that sheared at ninety degree angles and ran hundreds of feet up from the water abounded in Mendocino County, and if that weren't enough to do someone in, the rocks in the ocean and the chilly temperature would finish the job.

And if I kept thinking on this tangent, I would be at an uncontrollable level of fear again. So I sawed harder with my mini blade and tried to concentrate on the frustration of that job. Because I was trying to cut only the ropes and not my left hand, the angle at which my right hand held the knife was painful. Every few minutes I let the right hand rest. I switched hands, but my left hand had less staying power than the right. Saw and rest, saw and rest, switch hands, saw and rest. The monotony was broken only by the spurts of fear that crept in my thoughts if I didn't concentrate only on sawing.

"… bring her car back along here and push it over the edge. The body will be at one location and the car at another. It will be awhile before they're connected." Percival told his lover after they had stopped the car and were coming around the back to finish their task.

"She was smarter than you gave her credit for. She did-n't bungle it like you said she would," Percival said derisively.

"I didn't say that," Charles said without a whole lot of conviction.

"Yes, you did."

"No, I said she's too thorough and never has enough time to do everything as thoroughly as she'd like, so she gets behind. A new case would just throw her timing off more and rattle her, so she wouldn't see what was going on."

The key rattled the latch as it was inserted, the lid flipped up, and Percival reached down to pull me out of the trunk. He reached out to steady me after I—hands held behind my back—had flung my legs over the lip of the trunk. As he righted me, I screamed at him in my loudest school-marm voice, "Don't you dare touch me! I'll get out myself." It took him aback enough to make him stand still and allow me to tug my upper body straight with my hands still behind my back, the voluminous folds of the my skirt concealing my back. Percival stood slightly away from the back of the car, and Charles stood behind him off to the left. Knowing the tim-ing had to be right, I stood off to the right away from the back of the car. As Percival reached for me, I gripped the crowbar as hard as I could in my right hand, threw all my anger and body weight into the extended arm and slammed the left side of his face and head. The thud and loud crack of bone and the spreading darkness on his face told me the crowbar had avenged the killing of Leticia.

Charles crumpled to Percival's side and said, "Louisa, what have you done? I think you killed him!"

"Good," I said echoing the last thought Percival had said to me at the office.

"Where are the keys, Charles?" Holding the crowbar in front of me, I yelled again when he didn't answer, "Where are the keys, Charles?"

"What, Louisa? The keys? I don't know. In the car I think. But you aren't going to, I mean, Percival is dying. You can't leave him here to die. Don't leave, Louisa."

The man was sobbing. Tears running down his cheek looked like silver strings in the moonlight.

"Poor Percival ... You poor thing," he said as he cradled the top half of his lover's head with one hand while trying to connect the jaw half to the rest of his face with his other.

When I climbed into the driver's seat, I found the keys were in the ignition. I hit the doorlock button, so all four doors sealed me against Charles, put the car in gear and started to slide out of the turn out where Percival had parked.

Overdosed on adrenaline and disoriented, I didn't know where I was driving. As I approached Gualala, I knew I had to reverse directions and start heading south on Highway 1. Unless I got behind a waddling RV, I would probably be home within three to four hours. Although I've traveled Highway 1, I wasn't sure of where to cut over to Highway 101 until I could get further south, and I wasn't too keen on stopping to try to find a map in the car. Making a concerted effort to shut off my thinking about all that had happened that night, I concentrated only on getting home to Woofy. He hadn't had his walk and would know something was wrong. He'd probably be fearful of being forsaken again.

Light was just creeping up to open a new day when I

drove into my driveway. It's a calm feeling to arrive at my haven, but tonight the relief was so overwhelming I didn't notice until I got into the garage the lights on in the house. An unreasonable panic that Charles might have gotten there before me had me approaching the door very slowly. Woofy heard the car and shifted into a high-pitched, excited bark that made me even more cautious until I heard Emily tell him it was all right and to be quiet. Still he kept barking.

"Mom, are you okay?" asked a relieved Emily as I opened the door and knelt down to receive Woofy's tongue bath welcome.

"Yes. What are you doing here?"

Bob Washburn had stepped into the kitchen behind Emily, and Gen stood behind him. "And, what are you doing here?" I asked surprised to see them.

Emily said, "You missed dinner and didn't call. I thought when you were giving me your schedule, you were just being compulsive. When I didn't hear from you by 10:00, I called Lt. Washburn, and he didn't confirm my thoughts I was being silly. That worried me even more. So I came over here thinking you might have forgotten about dinner, except you weren't here either, so I started waiting."

"I went to your office, but no one was there," explained Bob. "I had the Pleasant Creek police contact the emergency numbers listed on the business license application. Genevieve here came over and let us in with her key. Your purse and sweater were still on the floor in Charles' office, and I realized what you had said about Percival the night we went to dinner was right. I figured you and Charles had been kidnapped by Mr. Hough-Streng, so we've been looking for you all over the county."

For once, Gen displayed her most quiet self as she stood there staring at me with a mixed expression of surprise, fear and concern.

"I haven't been in the county, and Charles and Percival are lovers. Charles was in on the whole thing. They're the ones who killed Leticia."

"Let me get you something to drink, so you'll relax and then give us the whole story," he said.

"Yes, but before I do that, Percival is lying on the side of Highway 1 with his face smashed in. Charles is there, and someone needs to get to them."

"Okay, relax, don't say a word until I call this in. We'll get someone out there. Who clobbered him, Louisa?" he asked although his tone told me he knew.

After he gave terse instructions and cryptic answers on the phone, he held the receiver and asked, "Where are they?"

"They are at a turnout which was where they were going to throw me down the cliffs into the ocean somewhere south of Gualala."

"Mother!" gasped Emily.

He repeated what I had said and ended the conversation with, "You'd better send several troopers along with the rescue squad."

And I began. I had expected to vent during the retelling of details. I had expected to emote in anger for Percival, in frustration with not seeing the complete puzzle, in pity for Mrs. Streng and Zoë and Charles, and in forgiveness for Leticia. I had thought the all-consuming fear I had experienced would provide more impetus for emotion. None of that happened. I told the story calmly and with very little expression as if I were hypnotically repeating instructions. I didn't even look at my listeners.

"Percival had decided to take his inheritance by little chunks before his mother died. He'd have services billed in lump sums, so he could send the claim to the insurance companies, and if he couldn't hit the insurance, he'd bill the trust. He'd tell the supplier it would be easier to get through channels in the insurance accounts payable department by billing all at once. Then he'd never bring his mother in for appointments, and, shortly after the services had started, he'd quit them. But he still had the insurance money because few companies are going to request an audit of attendance at appointments, and since he had cancelled all the succeeding appointments, he could pocket the money. The audiologist confirmed what I thought. They had a signed contract for hearing aids on a thirty-day trial for Mrs. Streng. Percival made sure the most expensive hearing aids were fit on his mother and had paid for the aids in full out of his mother's account, but he returned the aids and got most of his mother's money back. The attorneys and accountants of his mother's estate, should they ever ask about the appliances, would be told she was uncomfortable in wearing them, and they were lying in a drawer. Who would ever look? I would imagine Percival made a pretty substantial amount over the last few months. He was abusive to his mother, too. He may even have been the instigating factor in the onset of the stroke when he hit her. He does hit hard. Ask me how I know."

Gen moved toward me and put her hand on my shoulder. She continued to absently pat it as I gave them all the details of the previous evening. I still didn't fall apart. Very likely, when I was least expecting it, this unfound emotion would bubble to the surface and burst. I might be meeting with a client, speaking before a group, taking my granddaughters out, and I would become hysterical.

It wasn't the solitude that bothered me when I finally let my husband go. Solitude can become an elixir that allows one to catch oneself. Sit back, feet up and watch through half-closed eyes movements, reactions and words and reflect, recheck and reevaluate those situations and people with whom we have contact.

No, it wasn't the solitude. It was the lack of camaraderie which could easily lead to loneliness. I think that's probably the reason I tried to stay so busy, and, of course, by keeping busy, I was always late. By keeping busy, it was easier to focus outside one's self. But, that frenetic activity didn't completely cover the fact that there was no one to button the buttons on the back of my blouse, no one to tell me my roots were going gray and needed a dye job, no one to make a secret joke out of a faux pas. There was no intimate company anymore. I adjusted eventually; it wasn't as difficult as I had led myself over the years to believe it would be. Not having the companionship became a habit like most of our lifestyles. I still had hiccups of despair, but by keeping busy, I had moved on to a steadier keel.

None of us had said anything for about twenty minutes. I don't think any of us had even moved. The silence wasn't uncomfortable, so no one felt it needed to be interrupted.

It never occurred to any of us at work to think about Charles being lonely or needing a relationship of any kind. We all read him as being so keen on developing the agency, we never attributed to him the need for a private life. One realization of this situation was in how remiss it was of all of us to give Charles only a professional identity. I can't ever remember anyone saying "How are you?" to him. We never asked him how his weekend went. We knew very little about his family or background. There was no place on Charles' magnificently tailored suits to wear the insecurities and vulnerabilities each of us displayed in our own lives. He must have been a lonesome person, and none of us saw it.

Many of us can adjust to the alone times, but it can be frightening. I suppose Charles couldn't or didn't want to. Intimacy with one person must have been something he had little of in his lifetime. He was so afraid of losing that intimacy when he finally did discover it, that he could be led to desperate fear of the loss of Percival's love. Percival knew it well, having discovered Charles' need to be close to someone and mastered the manipulation of Charles. He had tried to manipulate Zoë, too, but she was stronger in that she had a safety net of support in her parents. She resisted much of Percival's control which must have increased his frustration and his cruelties to others. He either hid it from Zoë, or she chose not to see it.

Charles very much liked Leticia because she treated

the clients well. The torment of murdering her must have eaten at him, but not having Percival if he didn't do it would have been even worse.

"Come home, Mom. Come to our house," Emily kept saying.

"No, there's a visit I have to make. I'm okay now."

"I'll wait in the car."

"It may be awhile."

"I have a book. I'll wait."

Bob got up to leave, and, as I walked him to the door he said, "It wouldn't hurt you to stay with your daughter. It might be more relaxing, and I'd feel better about it."

"No, I need to see the Strengs, and then I need a couple days of sleep. I'll do that better here."

"I'll call you later," he said as he walked out my door.

Thirty Five

GEN WALKED OVER TO ME, PUT HER ARM AROUND ME and said, "Louisa, you are probably my oldest and dearest friend who understands me better than anyone. If I had lost your friendship tonight…" She finished with a muffled sob.

After I walked her to the door, she gave me a hug and said, "Now, Louisa, don't you dare be late on Monday morning!"

Emily packed me in her mini-van, and we drove. This time, the brown hills held no appeal even though I stared at them. Same color, same cows, same highway.

Emily asked if I was all right.

"You sure you want to go here? Tomorrow you might regret going there so soon after…"

My look must've told Emily that I was resolute.

She got quiet and continued to drive, but told me she was coming with me when we arrived at the Strengs. Zoë answered the door, but I didn't look at her as I told her I was going to see her mother and walked inside.

"Mrs. Streng, it's over. I'm so sorry about what's been happening, but it's over," I said to the woman in the bed. She seemed to shrivel even more as she melded into the bed like a melting ice cube. The woman had been pulverized by an evil son, wasted by a stroke, and risked being annihilated into a vapid shell if she didn't confront the circumstances now.

She pulled the sheet over her head with her functioning arm. I drew the sheet back off and heard both our daughters gasp, "Mother!"

Emily started to come at me, but surprisingly Zoë stopped her.

"Mrs. Streng, Marguerite, talk to me. They know about

179

Percival. We know what he's done and how he covered it up. Please talk to us now. I'm not trying to hurt you. I know you know what's going on. Talk to me."

She had crouched into a fetal, defenseless curl, her arm over her head. As I pleaded with her, she moved the arm slightly and peeked out.

"Please," I said.

Slowly, she took her communication board and pointed to the letter "I". As gently as I could, I took her board and bent it in half.

"No. You can talk. You've been able to since before Leticia died. Tell us what you know. You can't shut yourself from the world anymore. This community needs you. Zoë is going to need you. The agency very much needs you. You don't have to hide anymore."

She slinked down into the bedclothes to curl again. It took awhile. She hadn't organized thoughts or used her oral musculature for many weeks, and communication must have atrophied somewhat. When she did start talking, she sounded like an old 45 rpm record at 33 rpm speed. That and the slight drool she couldn't control out the immobile side of her face made it difficult to comprehend what she needed to say. Emily ransacked her purse for a tissue to give to Mrs. Streng. It added to her composure enough that she used it as a shield to cover her mouth while she droned out her story.

"Leticia and I used to talk about Percival when he wasn't around. One of the reasons she took me to my doctors was because he never would. I never told her about the stealing. She figured it out when he kept canceling doctors and reblitation, rehablation—no rehab."

"That's right," I said. "Re-ha-bil-i–ta-tion."

She repeated it and got it right.

"Leticia asked what I wanted her to do. I told her to do nothing. Percival would get mean and maybe hurt her. When she found out about him, I got mad at her. She told me I wasn't really mad at her, I was embrassss."

"Em-bar-rassed," I said.

Again she repeated the word.

"I thought about it. She was right. I was upset someone knew. I was trying to keep it a secret. I had kept his meanness a secret so long. Leticia was smart. She knew. Zoë knew some of what happened, but she acted like she didn't. Zoë thought I didn't know she knew. She tried to protect me. She still loved her big brother, though. And I don't think she saw everything. Zoë didn't know Leticia knew, and Zoë didn't quite know what Percival was doing. She just knew it was something not right. That's why she tried to be here as much as she could. That's why she would tell him to go see his friends. I thought he would get better. But he hadn't ever been better. When he was at school, he'd come home and each time he got more vulgar. I wasn't sure why.

"One time when he was in college, he came home and we got in an argument. I forget what about, but that's when he hit me the first time. He never said he was sorry. I never told his father. Paul, my second husband, was really his stepfather, but he treated Percival like his own son. That's what I didn't understand. I thought Paul would make up for his real father. Percival's father had been so distant when he was with us, and then he left. We never knew where he went."

She stopped because the effort of speaking was so hard and tiring for her. The three of us waited patiently because Mrs. Streng gave no indication she wished to quit talking.

She started up again, and her voice was stronger, "The best protection, especially after Leticia died, was to not talk. That way, Percival wouldn't hurt anyone around me. Since he thought I couldn't talk, he thought no one knew how he treated me."

She sat back on her pillow and closed her eyes.

With eyes still closed, she said, "My family always operated on the idea that social graces and manners would get one through any bad time. I tried with Percival to make that work for him and his life and mine. It didn't. He was one person for whom social graces were a loss."

With those words, she threw off the robe of the debilitated invalid and seemed to become stronger and taller as we observed her sitting upright in her bed.

"What do you mean 'they know about him?'" she asked when she recalled what I said.

Leaving out a few details, namely the crowbar, I told an abridged version of what had happened last night and left shortly after that. Neither woman asked as many questions as I thought they might. It was as though they knew Percival's life would come to some distasteful episode that would take him out of their lives. As Mrs. Streng talked, her voice, weakened by disuse and trepidation, became stronger and louder the more she explained. Whether or not she consciously realized it, she was losing not only the shackle created by her son, but also the bond to him. But I very much doubted either woman would want to deal with me in any way when they fully realized the role I played in rifting their family. Knowing I was the instrument that unchained them but also the reminder of the wasteful pain endured by them created a sadness for me because I had enjoyed the company of these two women.

Zoë alluded to it as we walked the luxury of the hallway.

"I've enjoyed working with you, Louisa. I don't know if we'll see each other again, but I will be grateful for what you did for Mother.

"And me," she said after a pause.

Epilogue

It WOULD NEVER MATTER TO PERCIVAL THAT HE WAS surrounded by the luxury of an exclusive psychiatric hospital and not the lackluster environment of the state mental institution. His psychopathic personality, now veneered by severe brain damage, would never allow him to recognize that the money he so coveted now paid for his care. He now had his share of his stepfather's money, and he would never know it. The Strengs' visits to him became more infrequent as time passed because there was no visible recognition of the two women on Percival's part.

Although Jill completed the file and paperwork on Mrs. Streng, Zoë requested of the agency that I work with her in the adoption proceedings of Ian. Zoë must have agreed with Mrs. Chu about Ian looking like an Ian because that is his Christian name, Ian Percival Streng. Zoë still permits her sisterly love to blind herself to Percival's savagery. Still quiet, but by choice, not environment, Ian is an alert and healthy young boy.

Allowing me to be a part of the adoption was a nice gesture on Zoë's part, and I was able to watch the recovery of Mrs. Streng at a distance. In spite of her leg brace and slightly slurred speech, she made an almost complete recovery in a few short weeks. She still sits on our Board of Directors for Community Action Group and has taken an active role in the search for a new executive director to replace Charles.

Ah, yes, Charles. Periodically I will drive to the prison to see him because he has no one else who will visit him. Sometimes Gen will go with me, but I don't ask her to go that often because, frankly, I would rather listen to nice music on the CD player than have her tell me what my co-workers and I have done wrong. Charles seems to enjoy our visits as a break in his routine, but, truth to tell, he seems satisfied with the niche he has carved for himself in the monotonous structure of prison life. During one visit he talked about Leticia and how he was infatuated with her beauty.

"One day I asked her to accompany me to dinner. I thought we could have a nice evening out, just dinner and conversation, nothing else. Do you know what she said?"

"No," I answered.

"She told me a price and said it had to be in cash. And, then she laughed and walked out."

"Charles, did you not see what she was telling you?"

"It appeared she didn't want to go with me. I guess she was trying to tell me the level of restaurant she wanted to dine at, and that was her way of saying she didn't want my company."

"Oh, Charles. She was a call-girl. That's how she made money. By all appearances, lots of it."

"But, I wasn't wanting to take her to bed."

"I know, Charles, I know."

We have an interim director at the agency. This week her hair is peach, an artifact of the crayon red hair she had sported. It seems her red dye didn't quite rinse out the week of Percival's 'accident', so her hairdresser slowly weaned her into another lighter color. Gen does surprisingly well as an executive director because her amazing ability to divest her co-workers of all pertinent facts about their lives and her aptitude at mental categorization of that information is just what she needs to keep on top of the Community Action Group.

Bob Washburn stopped by my house later in that traumatic week to take me to dinner and dancing. Surprised enough by his visit not to think about my greeting to him when I opened the door, I surprised both of us when I said, "Hi, Bubba!"

A long pause on his part created an uneasy silence in which I fervently wished I could rewind the moment to play it back differently.

When he did finally look at me with softened eyes, he said, "Yeah, that's okay."

MALINDA HALL has been a bookkeeper, speech therapist, and an English and math teacher. Besides enjoying writing, she says "The kids are wonderful, the husband is great, the dog is a kick, and life is fun."